ENCORE

CENTER STAGE BOOK TWO

REBECCA STONE

STARR STREET PUBLISHING

1

"Hi, my name is Gideon and I'm an alcoholic." The green chip was heavy in his hand. "Um. Well, I'm a touring musician and got back from an eight month tour not too long ago. Today marks three months sober." He looked at the chip in his hand, swallowing back the lump in his throat while he felt what the chip meant. "It's the longest I've ever gone, and probably the hardest thing I've ever done. Some days are easier than others. Thanks."

He walked back to his seat, head down while everyone clapped and thanked him.

Jesus fuck. Gideon hated the attention. He hated the confessions. He hated that he was still nervous to share his story. But he knew three months was a big deal. He sat, fingering his new coin while someone else started speaking. The coin's emerald color reminded him of Ella. He felt the tightness in his chest as his heart broke a little more.

His band, Eternal Youths, had been the opening act for an eight month national and world tour with the famous band, The National. He'd tried drowning himself in every vice he could, just to rid himself of her. The glow of her blonde hair in the morning sun peeking through her bedroom window. The way her smile lit every room she entered. The scent of vanilla and sandalwood resting on her skin. The look on her face when he'd broken his word, sipping whiskey from a flask offered by his cousin, his bandmate. The sound of her voice telling him he needed to figure out his relationship to alcohol without her.

Sometimes the distractions on tour worked. Most times they didn't. There were nights he couldn't remember, blurred pieces of memory that randomly appeared. A brunette's naked backside. Tumbled over shot glasses. Hand pressed against a wall, the sidewalk spinning beneath him.

"Hey, Pike, congrats." The voice shook him from his thoughts, and he looked up to see his sponsor Amy standing in front of him, her dark skin glowing under the yellow lights. She had a habit of calling him by his last name; it always made him feel like they were in battle together. The meeting had ended and everyone had moved to the refreshments in the back.

"Thanks, Amy. Couldn't have gotten here without you picking up the phone at 3 a.m." He stood, shoving his hands in his pockets while he followed her to the back.

"My pleasure." She laughed, flashing him a smile. Her two years sober helped motivate him, and her work as a sound engineer in the music industry helped support him. They joined a group around the pastry table, Amy piping in with her standard animation. Gideon shifted on his feet. He thought he'd had trouble opening up before being sober, but this was another level. He was still adjusting to having the crutch of alcohol removed, and he enjoyed being alone that much more.

The group laughed at something, and he smiled. Tried to fit in. Everything was a little brighter than it'd been before, these human moments more brilliant in all their color. One by one the group started leaving, and he waved a goodbye before making his own exit. The September air was crisp, the passing cars bringing a breath of autumn on the cool breeze. He was lucky the church that held the AA meetings was only a fifteen minute walk from his apartment in the quaint college town of Sugar Grove, New York.

His upbringing in New York City, just two hours south of his new home, had given him his love of music with it's bright lights and never-ending traffic. While he sometimes missed the buzz of the big city, he enjoyed the aloneness afforded by the night stars and distant laughter of people finding themselves. He started walking home, enjoying the stillness and contemplating how to translate it into a song.

He didn't know how long he'd been walking when a laugh rang out, and he froze.

He knew that laugh.

He'd dreamt about that laugh.

That laugh haunted him, day in and day out.

He looked across the street, realizing how far he'd walked when he saw the small Mediterranean restaurant a block from his apartment. The blonde head thrown back under the lit awning stole his breath. Her laugh filled the night air, a song all its own. Gideon felt the pit in his stomach turn to stone, the nausea rising in his throat. His heart raced. He couldn't stop staring, trying to ignore the two hand-some men she was laughing with.

And then she turned.

Her smile disappeared at the sight of him, and they held each other's gaze across the street, the cars between them a blur.

With her, the world around them had always been a blur.

A bus rattled down the road between them. After it passed he saw her enter the restaurant, her hand pulling one of the men with her, the other following closely behind.

And then she was gone.

2

The computer screen stared back at her, the Instagram page still not updated.

Ella Davis had just short of stalked Gideon on social media since they parted ways a year ago. But once his band's headlining tour with The National ended three months ago, he'd gone dark.

Not that the pictures from tour left anything to the imagination.

She'd seen the girls and drinks and heard the drunk after-party videos.

That was enough for her to try and scrub him from her mind, even though they'd agreed to keep the door open and see how things were when he came back. But it was clear he hadn't changed. And if that was who she'd seen when she was out with her friend Ben and his brother Nick, that meant Gideon was back in town and hadn't told her.

I guess he also scrubbed me from his mind.

She sighed, closing out of the tab on her browser and returning to her notes. She needed to focus. After their success last year with a local band they were able to help get signed and on tour, Ella and her business partner Rachel had been able to travel the country and meet with interested parties. The local band, ADAC, hadn't been shy in promoting their success and attributing most of it to Maven Media, the company Ella and Rachel ran together. Rachel was out of town with their paralegal friend Julie, working on sealing a new band client, and Ella had a big call with a small publishing company based out of New York City. If they landed both accounts their small media and publicity company could make the move to the Big Apple.

Shit.

She'd lost track of time, scrambling to get her notes together in the two minutes left before the call, silently cursing herself for letting the guy who'd broken her heart distract her yet again. She switched to muttering her new last name, her grandmother's maiden name a foreign feel on her tongue. After Gideon had caught onto who she was last year, she'd changed her name professionally from Ella Davis to Ella Thompson. It was an attempt to distance herself from her slightly less than famous parents, two leading actors whose fame had brought them a dependency on alcohol, a failed marriage, and a single daughter. The bitter custody battle when Ella was a baby had been fairly public, and she wanted to make it as difficult as possible for clients to figure out who she was.

She checked the time, dialing the number a few minutes after their the scheduled meeting time.

"Hi, Charlie? This is Ella Thompson with Maven Media, how are you?"

When the other woman replied, her voice was low and raspy. It reminded Ella of her mom, Margaret, who she'd been able to convince some-what recently to try rehab again. Ella had gone into this business, publicity and crisis management for the arts, after seeing her mother fail to get cast because of her ability to drain bottles. Some days were easier than others. Today was not one of those days. She stood to ease some of her tension, moving through the conversation pleasantries before getting to business.

"I'm so glad we were able to connect, I'm sorry my business partner Rachel can't join us this time.

We loved receiving your email and understand how hard it can feel to juggle so many authors in a variety of genres. At Maven Media, we create tailored brands and campaigns for each talent so you can focus on what you do best." She sounded like a billboard as she walked to one of the two windows in her small office, laughing at Charlie's exasperated agreement.

"It's hard out there!" Ella said. "We understand you're looking to hire freelance publicists and media marketers for up to twenty individual brands, is that correct?" She turned from the window, pacing the room while Charlie confirmed her needs. The small office held two desks by the window, and a small love seat and coffee table sat across from the door for when she and Rachel needed a change of scenery.

"That's perfect," Ella said. "I sent you the rate sheet, did you have any questions regarding that or when you'd like to start?" She turned around and headed to her desk, needing a sheet of paper and a pen.

"The retainer is paid at the start of the month," she said, shuffling her papers to find Rachel's notes on the outline for retainers versus individual management. She looked up when she heard the door open, the papers in her hand falling to the floor.

Gideon.

Ella swallowed, alarm coursing through her body, her skin heating with a love mingled with hate. He shouldn't be here. And he especially shouldn't look so good.

His dark hair still fell in those ocean blue eyes. He was leaner, but his broad shoulders pulled at his suit jacket the way she remembered, the white button-down hinting at the delicious chest she'd memorized. His hands were in the pockets of his black jeans, the sleeves rolled up to show the tattoos along his forearms, the inky lines disappearing beneath the fabric. She knew they wrapped around his biceps. Those big, strong...

"Hello?" Charlie's voice cut through her thoughts, and she realized she'd stopped mid-sentence.

"Oh, I'm so sorry, Charlie. I spilled something. Yes, I heard you loud and clear, I can send over a contract for review as soon as we hang up." Her voice had cracked, and she stooped to the papers, trying to find the right one while hiding her face from the one person she couldn't live without but never wanted to see again. She found the right paper, reading it through blurred eyes. "Oh, yes. I apologize, the retainer would be in your best interest as it covers a broader scope of tasks for all the talent. If you went for the individual management, you'd have to pay for each talent and since it's publicity, anything could come up at any time for any one of them." Ella wiped her face while Charlie went over some of her more problematic authors. Ella took a deep breath as she scooped up the papers, standing to put them on her desk. Gideon stood directly in front of her, and she jumped at his sudden nearness, the smell of him she had hoped to forget. She turned, hoping to remove his assault on her senses so she could stop making an ass of herself to Charlie.

She needed to focus. She needed this account.

They needed this account.

"Okay, great," Ella said. "I'll send that to you this evening. Thank you so much, Charlie, it was a pleasure."

Ella hung up and took a deep breath. The initial shock of seeing Gideon had now clamped an iron case over her heart.

All those tears she'd cried.

All the nights he'd haunted her dreams.

And now here he stood, in her office, the one person she'd never been able to let go.

3

Fuck.

He'd forgotten what it felt like to be so close to her.

"Ella." Even her name on his lips felt like a missing puzzle piece, and his heart started hurting all over again when she didn't respond. He fingered the green chip in his jean pocket, the ridges a familiar comfort.

"Ella, please."

He watched her head fall, shoulders sagging as she turned to face him. Her eyes met his, and he felt his knees go weak. The other half of his soul stood before him, and judging by the look on her face, she felt the same.

"What are you doing here?" Her voice wavered and she crossed her arms. He recognized her need for security and hated himself for being the one to cause it.

"I - I needed to see you."

The tension in the air changed as Ella scoffed, looking him up and down.

"Are you kidding me right now?" Her eyes held a fire he hadn't seen in forever, and fuck if he didn't want to apologize by worshiping every inch of her golden body. "You've been back for three months and now you come running? Fuck that, Gideon. That's not how this works."

Her words stung, but he deserved so much worse. She uncrossed her arms and walked around him, the wide arc avoiding him at all costs. Yeah, that was a bit worse. Her heels sank into the carpeted floor as she made her way to the door. He'd always loved watching her walk, and the tight pencil skirt only highlighted her gorgeous curves. He remembered how they overflowed in his hands. Her hair had gotten longer since he last saw her, the blond layers swishing with every step she took. She turned to face him, her eyes hard when they met his.

"It's time for you to leave." She opened the door.

He watched her, surprised by the fierce woman before him. This was not the girl he'd left a year ago. So help him, her strength made him fall for her even harder. He could only hope she'd give him a chance. He opened his mouth to explain, but knew nothing he said would be enough. The look in her eyes was clear. No matter what happened next, he had hurt her more than could easily be forgiven.

Challenge accepted.

He'd become the man she deserved, and he'd show her that. He took his time, walking and holding her gaze until he was directly in front of her, her chest rising and falling, so close it almost brushed his. Vanilla infiltrated his nostrils, and he leaned closer without breaking the distance. The door creaked as she leaned on it for balance, and a different aroma rose to his nose.

Holy hell, she was wet.

Those petal lips parted while her cheeks flushed, green eyes softening while they searched his. Even in heels, his body completely covered hers. His recent gym exploits in lieu of alcoholic drinks might've helped with that, which made the need to hold her even greater. To feel her softness against his body.

Oh, yeah. Now he remembered what it was like being so close to her.

"As you wish." He whispered into her neck, lips brushing her skin with words from her favorite movie. Words with a hidden promise. He left a breath of a kiss on her most sensitive area before walking out the door. It took everything in him to not look back, especially after the soft gasp his kiss had elicited.

If he was going to win her back, it wasn't going to be today.

4

The small sofa in her office would never provide the support she needed after a move like that.

Head in her hands, Ella tried to steady her breathing. Gideon had only been there for a few minutes, but it was enough to undo almost all the "letting go" she had convinced herself she'd done. She was shaking, more from the fire he lit in her core than from the anger she felt at seeing him.

Of course he'd pulled one of her all-time favorite movie lines.

Of course he'd stood close enough to touch her but not actually do so.

Of course he knew she still loved him.

Being that close to him had made everything else disappear, and the old feeling of being able to handle anything so long as they were together came flooding back. Except she had to remind herself that wasn't the case, as they had so clearly experienced last year when he tried to quit drinking and couldn't. She hated that it was his crutch. But even more so she hated that she hadn't been enough, an expectation that could only ever bring pain.

And why would he dare come back after three months of radio silence? Some things were better left alone. Her heart was one of them. After he went on tour, she'd tried to see other people. But the small town of Sugar Grove and shattered state of her heart didn't lend itself well to recovery, and after a couple months she'd put that on hold. She'd delved into the business until it occupied every free moment. Rachel was talking about moving downstate to New York City; after Ella saw Gideon had come back but hadn't reached out, she worked even harder to make that dream come true.

Ella clenched her thighs, trying to reconcile how someone she loved so much could evoke so much hate. She picked at her nails, a bad habit she'd formed when Gideon first left for tour and the pictures posted online had depicted her every fear. She tried to calm herself from the memories of him. Of the way his arms felt around her, the way his hips moved against hers. The things his mouth could do. The words he used to whisper to her. She hadn't been touched, hadn't been loved, in so long, and he was the last person who needed to reintroduce her to that. She decided some meditation breathing exercises could help. She kicked off her heels and sat at her desk, using the mala her mom had gifted her for her birthday as a guide.

In. Out. In. Out.

Beloved... Gideon... Asshole... Okay, that's not very meditative, relax...

In. Out. In. Out.

Goddammit.

She opened her eyes and sighed. Her body was still buzzing from her encounter. Sure, meditation was exactly what she should be doing to calm herself. But she really just wanted to throw something at the wall and scream. Ella stood, ready to do just that when Rachel walked in.

"Hey!" Rachel threw her a quick smile as she set her bag on the couch and took off her heels.

"Hey, how was the trip?" Ella asked, her voice foreign to her own ears. Rachel looked up, her face wary. Standing, Rachel was basked in the sunset glow streaming through the windows while she smoothed the front of her tailored cream sheath dress, no doubt a Chanel original, given her CEO-father's connections and wealth. Her long, dark brown hair was tousled, offsetting the structure of the dress. Despite having the face and body of a model, Rachel was one of the most genuine, kind people Ella had ever met.

"It was amazing, they want to sign a contract by end of next week. How was the call with Charlie?" She padded over barefoot to Ella's desk and sat on the corner. Ella was a little concerned she'd messed up the call at the end, what with Gideon showing up out of nowhere. While the business and their mutual friend Julie had brought Ella and Rachel closer, she wasn't sure she was ready to tell Rachel about Gideon's untimely comeback. Or her less than professional behavior on the call.

"It was good! She was sorry you weren't there, but she's thinking the monthly retainer to cover all their authors makes the most sense. I'm going to send over the contract Julie helped with and Charlie said she'd look it over."

"Hmmm, anything else, El?" Rachel's dark brown eyes pierced Ella's, who felt her face flush in response. Her pale skin had never been good at helping her hide anything, and of course it'd kick into gear now.

"Nope, that's it." She looked away, trying to focus on the contract she needed to send.

"El. I saw him. Gideon, on the street."

Ella's fingers stopped moving, the computer screen going out of focus as she tried to catch her breath. It was one thing for Ella to speak of him, a ghost. But it was different when someone else formed the letters of his name, each breath causing her heart to tighten. She'd thought she'd reached the place of being okay when she heard his name from someone else's lips.

Wrong.

She looked up at her friend, unsure where to start. She wanted to burst into tears and be held. She wanted to yell and curse and to start her mission of throwing things. She wanted him to not affect her this way. Rachel just looked at her, waiting.

"It's kind of a long story," Ella whispered.

"I've got time. We're friends, right?"

Rachel was right. Ella sighed, pulling her friend to the sofa so she could let her in.

5

The rehearsal room was more stifling than usual, and Gideon had to stop himself from grabbing a cold beer from the mini fridge their manager, Tom, kept stocked. Gideon knew their ability to go on a headlining tour next year rested on the new album they were working on. Which meant, as the primary songwriter of the band, it was almost entirely up to him to make sure it happened.

The guys milled about, working with the new lyrics Gideon had brought in. Their drummer Lucas sat in his seat, his top bun moving with each tap of his kit while Ryan worked the bass. His cousin Anthony, the one who'd handed him that flask all those months ago, held his guitar, chewing his bottom lip while he looked over the words.

"Hey, Gideon? I need a word." Tom's voice startled Gideon back to the present, and he looked up to see his uncle, his manager, standing before him.

"Sure thing." He stood, following Tom out into the hallway of the rehearsal space. They squared off just outside the doors, and Gideon felt his arms cross out of reflex. After his dad passed away when he was a kid, Tom had stepped in as a semi-parental figure and tried to reign in Gideon's drug and alcohol use. Gideon was used to being defensive, but since losing Ella and being sober, he was trying to fix his automatic attitude. He relaxed his arms and looked into Tom's eyes.

"I know you've been through a lot, and I'm really proud of you. The road you've taken hasn't been easy. I wanted to check in, make sure everything was okay." Tom's eyebrows drew together. He opened his mouth, closing it and shaking his head.

"Yeah, man, thanks. I'm doing good." Gideon looked at his uncle. Something was wrong.

"Well, um, the lyrics you brought in will need some fixes, they're missing some of the spark from the first album, but I think they'll work."

Gideon nodded. Of course the lyrics weren't as good as before. Ella had been his driving force, his inspiration. He'd had the world with her, and had wanted to give it in return. But he'd failed, and she'd left. He fingered the green chip in his pocket, a constant reminder of where he was heading. And he wasn't going to let his uncle get off so easily.

"Sorry about the lyrics. Is there something else you wanted to talk about?"

Tom sighed, running his hand through his graying hair. "No, not really. Could you... Could you just keep an eye on Anthony for me?"

Well, Gideon hadn't expected that. "Yeah, of course." He softened, putting a hand on his uncle's shoulder. "I mean, he seems okay."

Tom looked away, trying to hide a sniff. "Yeah, I just worry about him, you know? In any case, let's work on those lyrics, get some of the fire back in you." His glassy eyes turned to Gideon, a forced smile on his face. He clearly didn't want to talk about his son, so Gideon wasn't going to push. At least not now.

"Yeah, sorry about that. You know, with Ella gone and all..." He shifted on his feet, breaking his gaze.

"Hey, I get it. When you find that special person, every action you do is born out of love for them. Anthony's mom? When I was with her, the sun was always shining. Try doing these actions out of love for yourself while you heal. We'll work on these lyrics as a group, they're a good base." Tom's voice was scratchy with emotion, and he clapped a hand on Gideon's shoulder before walking back into the room.

Gideon mulled over his uncle's words. That's how he'd always felt when he was with Ella, like the sun was always shining. Growing up with his cousin Anthony had meant growing up with Anthony's parents until their divorce when they were both eighteen. He saw what Tom meant. After his wife left, Tom had mourned alone, leaving Anthony to become Gideon's constant party companion. Tom had eventually pulled himself together, and that led to the band forming. The band had become everyone's family, and they loved each other in the same way; everything they did was out of love for one another. Gideon couldn't love Ella properly until he loved himself. But he could at least try to fix what he'd broken until he became the man she deserved.

He ran his hands through his hair, racking his brain for an idea that could reach her. He looked up as Anthony came through the door, leaning on the jamb.

"Hey man, what's up? Little lady got you all tied up?" Anthony flashed his Tom Cruise smile, knowing the answer already.

"I just don't know what to do. I need her."

"Yeah…" Anthony walked to his other side and leaned against the wall with him. "I'm sorry, man. You need to Lloyd Dobbler the situation. 'Cause dude, we need your old lyrics back."

"Who's Lloyd Dobbler?" Gideon looked at his cousin. The name sounded familiar, but he couldn't place it.

Anthony looked at him in mock horror. "You don't know Lloyd Dobbler? Gideon, he's literally been setting the precedent for how to treat a woman since the 80s. He's cinema royalty."

Ella. Of course that's where he'd heard the name from. She loved movies, and especially anything with romance. He'd never been super into movies, but since being back from tour he'd tried to expand on his cinematic education. He must've missed that one. He looked at Anthony, ready to ask where he could watch this movie. Anthony arched an eyebrow and crossed his arms.

"I own it, it was one of my mom's favorites. Come over tonight, we'll watch it." He walked back into the rehearsal room, and Gideon heard the guys laughing and shouting out ideas for the new song.

For the first time in a year, he felt hopeful.

6

"Ew, Julie, stop!" Ella shrieked and covered her eyes from the unfortunate online dating mess that was Julie's phone. She really didn't need to see a bunch of random guys' dicks. Even if they were a nice distraction from the one she wanted most.

Julie rolled onto her back, laughing hysterically. Since they'd become close friends in college with very busy schedules, they got together for Girl's Night every two weeks, takeout and boxed-wine style. They were going to start including Rachel, but for their last hurrah before that they decided to go old school and create a pallet of pillows and blankets on the floor of Ella's apartment. Julie finally calmed down, her panting still laced with a hint of a chuckle.

"Seriously, I'm happy for you. But I *really* don't

need to be included in your exploits." Ella took a sip of wine, turning her attention to the bad horror movie on the TV screen. Julie sat up, picking up a dumpling from the feast laid between them. Ella caught a wave of wasabi and soy sauce as Julie dipped the dumpling.

"Okay, but I also know how you are about Gideon. And I know you say he has a God Penis, so I'm trying to help you find another God Penis," Julie said through a mouthful of dumpling. "I clearly have plenty to share."

Ella laughed at her friend while she ate her greasy chicken lo mein, grateful for her almost-lawyer friend for making light of the situation. "You're not wrong. The third from last dick pic was definitely something write home about."

"Over my dead body would I ever tell my mom about my sex life. You know how disappointed she'd be in her little girl." Julie shook her head, eyes trained on the movie. Ella watched her friend before refilling their wine glasses.

She did know. Julie's parents were strict and had certain expectations of their beautiful blonde baby. While Julie fit their want of a stable job by going to law school, she decided to relieve some of the stress through guys. She didn't want anything serious, choosing to focus on her own happiness before someone else's. Sometimes things were a one-night make out in a bar, sometimes they lasted a couple months, sometimes they stayed friends. Like her fling with Gideon's lead guitarist, Anthony. Although it had ended when they went on tour, they still texted regularly.

"Ya know, I still can't believe Gideon had the audacity to show up at your office. Like, balls, man. BALLS." Julie could barely be understood over the next dumpling she'd shoved in her mouth.

"I'm more wondering if he's dumb or if he's stupid. What did he honestly think was going to happen?" Ella took a large drink from her glass. Yeah, seeing him had almost re-broken her heart. But it also angered her that he'd thought he could come back after everything.

"True." Julie paused. "El, you know it's okay to miss him, right?" Ella could feel her friend watching her, and she knew her face had betrayed her conflicted emotions.

"I know. But I'm also pissed and hurt and thanks to your strong 'boss woman' pep talks, I know better than to give him another chance. So I can miss him from afar, and that's enough." She hoped it actually was enough and downed her drink, reaching for the box. She'd always had conflicting emotions about drinking, and Gideon hadn't helped. She allowed herself to drink whatever and however much she wanted on special occasions and this one night every two weeks. A fourth glass wasn't going to kill her.

"Okay, but if you ever want to talk, I'm here for you. Oh my God, why did we pick this movie? Plants, seriously? We should've known what we were getting into with Mahky Mahk." Julie's faux Boston accent was always spot on, and Ella laughed.

"We chose it *because* it has him. We knew exactly what we were getting ourselves into." As the end credits rolled, Ella flipped back to the home screen to find a feel-good show she could leave on as background noise. Julie stood, clearing their dishes to the kitchen.

"Here, let me help." Ella rose to help, not quite as gracefully as she would've liked. They stood in silence by the counter, packing food and washing dishes. Ella was sure if they spoke, there would be a slur somewhere in there.

"Do you hear that?" Julie turned to her friend.

Ella turned the water off, straining to hear through the buzz in her head and the murmur of the TV.

Plink... Plink... Plink...

The girls looked at each other before heading to one of the windows in the living room, throwing it open to the cool fall air.

And to one of Ella's favorite songs.

Her jaw dropped at the sight below her. Gideon was standing on the edge of the sidewalk with a speaker in one hand, pebbles in the other. His inspiration was clear. She felt her heart swell while she listened to the song.

"Oh... my... God," Julie whispered beside her. "He remembered."

Ella couldn't help but smile, no matter how hard she told herself to not give him the satisfaction. But there he was, the only man she'd ever loved, playing her favorite song in a recreation from one of her favorite movies. She almost didn't care that he'd shown up at her office, that he hadn't called when he'd gotten back.

He was here now, and it was clear as broad daylight where he stood.

7

His hand had dropped the pebbles some time ago, using both hands to hold the speaker above his head while the song played out. She was his Juliet, and he would do whatever it took to be with her again.

Julie stepped back from the window so it was just the two of them. Gideon and Ella. He was mesmerized by the glow of the light cast on her head, giving her the halo he always saw above her. Her face had broken out in a smile she kept trying to hide. He knew if he was going to get her to listen, now was the time. As the song wound down, he lowered his arms and cleared his throat, taking a deep breath.

"Ella... I didn't reach out when I got back because I needed to get my head on straight. Please, give me a chance." His voice rang strong but slightly desperate, and he saw the hurt flash across her face, mimicking his own.

"I've heard that before, Gideon. I don't want..."

"I'm in AA."

The weighted silence between them filled the air. He saw the tension ease from her shoulders as she processed what he'd said. He'd wait all night if it meant hearing her voice one more time.

"You... You are?" Her voice crossed the space between them, small and unsure. But tinged with hope. He knew the admission might have that effect, and he only shared it because he knew he was there to stay. He had no intention of playing her heart, of taking her on another emotional roller coaster.

"Yeah, I am. Three months sober now." He fished in his pocket for his green chip, holding it up as high as he could for her to see.

She didn't respond. Gideon felt his heart clench with the fear it wasn't enough. That it'd never be enough. He set the speaker down and moved closer to the building.

"Coffee, tomorrow. Lunch, whatever you want. Let me just tell you where my head's at," he said.

And my heart.

He gazed up at her, watched her shift her weight and uncross her arms.

"Okay," she said. "Tea and Me at 1 p.m."

She turned and disappeared from the window. Julie came back into frame, shutting it with a thud, leaving Gideon on the empty street. He knew the hope of her returning was just out of reach but stared up anyway. He sent a whispered, "Thank you," to the closed window before turning to pick up his speaker. He threw one last longing glance at where his heart lived before heading to his car a few blocks down. Standing solo on the street, the car was easy to spot, moonlight highlighting the wear and tear on its shell. He hadn't bothered getting a new one since he rarely drove and it worked fine enough. The door squeaked as he climbed in, throwing the speaker on the passenger's seat.

Gideon couldn't believe his luck. In the three months he'd been sober and attending meetings, he'd learned a lot about forgiveness for himself. His sponsor Amy had answered many a call, talking him through the feelings of regret and shame he felt on a daily basis. She'd helped him not only see that he was human, but to feel it. That it was okay to make mistakes and to forgive himself. And to earn back the trust and respect of those he'd hurt. He just never thought he'd be lucky enough to have those people actually forgive him. He knew how much he'd messed up. He knew the people he hurt and the things he'd done.

Ella also knew those things, and she was giving him a chance to come clean. Gideon knew it would be dangerous to hope for anything more than this one conversation, but he couldn't stop himself for dreaming. He rested his forehead on the steering wheel, closing his eyes and inhaling the scent of leather, wishing it was her he was breathing in. Vanilla and sandalwood. Sunshine and home. The feel of her curves in his arms, her lips soft and full against his own. He sighed and started the car. His dreams would be better had in his bed.

8

The coffee grounds were everywhere. Ella had accidentally dropped the just-filled and unused portafilter on the counter at her part-time job of barista extraordinaire at The Lava Java. The coffee grounds, being to the coffee industry the way glitter was to the craft industry, decided to fall into every nook and cranny. She started remaking the latte, thankful it was a slow morning and the customer was distracted by something their friend had said. Gideon was under her skin again, at home inside her despite all the effort she'd done to keep him out. She set the finished drink in front of the girl before cleaning up the mess she'd made. She felt like she'd spent her life cleaning up messes, and she was tired.

"Hey, Ella Bella!"

She smiled at the familiar voice. Ben had

become her friend through this job she'd started almost two years prior, and she considered him almost like a brother. She faced him.

"Hey, Benji. You're early, couldn't wait to smell like pumpkin spiced lattes?" She finished wiping the short part of the L-shaped counter, moving to the employee desk hidden behind the stem of the L to give him a hug. He was early for his shift and had flung his backpack on the shared work space. He pushed his floppy brown hair out of his face, giving her a lopsided smile with his hug.

"You know I love the smell of PSLs. I know I'm early, I'm just gonna hang out here for a little, if that's alright."

"Of course. How are things?" Ella asked as she sat in the chair beside the one he claimed.

"Eh, they're good. Thankful it's my last year of grad school, I love reading but this Tolstoy is killing me." He heaved a copy of *War and Peace* on the desk, shaking his head. Reading was one of the things they bonded over, and they'd had many a spirited debate on the merits of Anna Karenina. "How are you, El?"

"I'm good, business is good," she said, looking in his puppy-dog eyes. "Gideon's back."

His mouth dropped.

"Like, back as in he contacted you?"

Having a guy friend that was practically a brother was a blessing. Ella caught Ben up, anxious for his opinion. She was meeting Gideon after her shift and, while she felt good and strong, she knew it never hurt to have the support of her close friends.

"Wow. Um... I mean, how do you feel? What do you want from him?" Ben asked.

She mulled over his words, picking at her nails.

"I'm anxious. I don't want to miss him like I do. Especially since it sounds like he's trying."

"Yes, but isn't there a rule in the program about no romantic relationships for some time?" Ben cocked his head, his gaze never leaving hers.

Oh. He was right. It was her turn for her mouth to drop. Ella couldn't believe she'd forgotten that very tiny, very important rule. With all the times her mom had gone to rehab or done programs for alcoholism, she should've remembered the twelve month rule.

"Uh, yes. Yes, there is. I completely forgot. So I guess it doesn't really matter what I want, he said he's been in the program for three months. So he has another nine of being uninvolved." She shook her head, looking up as the door jingled. She hopped up to take care of the new customers, suddenly realizing she needed to let everything go. There were things beyond her control, especially with Gideon, and especially with this newly remembered information. Ella took the drink orders and got to work. She needed to rethink how she was going to handle this meeting with the one man who'd made her feel alive. This one man who missed her, wanted her, needed her as badly as she did him.

But the decision had been made for them, and there was nothing Ella could do but let it play out.

9

Gideon looked up at the little white cottage at the top of the hill. Set back from the road, it came complete with a quintessential picket fence and gravel walkway. Tea and Me, a place he'd always overlooked, was on one of the small side streets in Sugar Grove and was perfect for weekend events or tea parties. And apparently trying to win back the heart of the woman he'd lost.

He made his way up to the porch of the refurbished house, wiping his feet on the door mat while he read it: "*Front Porch Sittin', Sweet Tea Sippin'.*" He chuckled. This was exactly the kind of place Ella would like.

He opened the door to a narrow hostess podium and no one standing behind it. The place was small with carefully placed tables that made use of the space but still felt private. It was mostly empty, a few couples scattered around the edges of the room. He didn't see Ella. He heard a hearty laugh before a door in the back flew open. A short woman came toward him, beaming through the white dust on her round face. He couldn't tell if her hair was graying or just made of flour. Gideon smiled back at this woman radiating warmth and memories of home-made chocolate chip cookies.

"Hello, dear. How can I help you?" she said as she attempted to straighten her appearance, only to make it worse.

"Hi, I'm meeting someone but she's not here yet."

"Oh, you must be Gideon. Ella told me to watch for you. Come with me." She turned and walked towards a second door in the back of the building. Gideon followed her through the frame and into a much larger room with a few big tables spread out, perfect for client dinners or parties. A couple smaller tables broke up the terrain. A blonde sat at one of them, head bowed to her phone.

"Hey, honey. He's here," the woman said as Ella looked up. To Gideon, the woman whispered, "You can take a seat, I'll be back in a few minutes." Before she left, she patted his shoulder in a way that made him miss his mom.

Gideon inched his way to the table. He'd dreamt about this moment, but nothing had prepared him for the anxiety or fear he now felt. He didn't know how she felt, what she wanted. He sat across from her, taking in her straight hair and green eyes. God, he'd missed those eyes. His heart lurched when she gave him a small smile.

"Hi, Gideon."

"Hi, Ella. Thanks." He looked around the room. "For this. For everything."

"Maggie will be back soon, I was thinking we could just get the Rose Cardamom pot? I'm not too hungry but if you wanted a treat..." She held his gaze. There was an air of confidence to her that she hadn't had before he'd left, and it made him want her even more. To learn this new woman who stood in place of the one he'd fallen in love with.

"I'm not hungry either." He threw her a smile of his own while the woman, Maggie, came back. She'd successfully wiped the flour from her face, and while she had fixed the stray hairs flying out of her pony-tail, her hair was still covered in a fine coating of dust.

"Hi, dears. What'll you have?" She stood with one hand supporting herself on the back of Ella's chair, the other resting on her hip. Her smile was genuine and soft while she looked between them.

"Maggie, we'll just have the Rose Cardamom pot." Ella looked adoringly at her friend while Maggie's face sported a look of shock.

"Well, I'd never! No treats? You always eat me out of house and home when you're here." Maggie looked at Gideon. "Did you hear that? I count on her and now what'll I do?"

Gideon couldn't help but laugh, especially when Maggie broke her act and smiled, shaking her head and muttering how crazy the whole scene was as she left them alone. Ella had joined Gideon in laughing.

"She's crazy, I'm sorry. She's a good friend of Rachel's so we come here often," she said, her laughter subsiding. He missed the sound as soon as it was gone. It rang through the cavernous room and filled a sliver of the hole she'd left. He smiled in return, knowing they couldn't avoid the elephant in the room forever. And while he wished he had a couple fingers of whiskey, neat, he'd drink as much Rose Cardamom tea as he could if it meant being close to her again.

10

Ella shifted in her seat, taking in the handsome man before her. His face was clear. Healthy. His arms were more pronounced as he rested them on the table top. His shirt pulled on his shoulders. She couldn't stop the flush of heat between her thighs, remembering him above her. Under her. She swallowed, straightened, ready to turn her mind from him and to the matter at hand. Maggie came in with their order.

"I'm sorry to bother you kids, here's your tea." She flashed Ella a quick glance while setting the tray on the table. "Just give a holler if you need anything, that's how my family usually calls for me." She winked at Gideon and shuffled out, leaving a trail of flour footprints in her wake. Gideon lifted the delicate china teapot, so small in his large hands, and poured her tea before his. He set it down and took a sip from his matching cup. He peered at Ella over the rim, his baby blues just as deep as before. She felt her guard slip and the whisper of her heart falling for him.

"So," he said, his voice wavering.

"So. How was the tour?" Ella had seen every picture, watched every video, but he didn't need to know that.

Gideon took another sip and looked away.

"It was... enlightening." He cleared his throat. "The traditional rockstar life isn't for me." His eyes met hers, vulnerable to her opinion. Her judgement. She took a deep breath, folding her arms on the table.

"Is that why you joined AA?" She tried to keep her voice stable, knowing that this delicate situation needed someone to be strong. Even if it meant fighting the urge to hold him, forgive him now that he claimed he'd changed.

"Part of it. I..." He placed his hands, open, on the table between them. "I needed help. I tried to drown out losing you and it made it worse. So much of it was a blur and we had several nights that I wish I could forget. It didn't make sense to go in the program before tour, but as soon as we got back Tom gave us a month to recuperate and I used it to join and get sober. It's been three months. I'm clean. And I'm so sorry for hurting you."

Ella looked down at his open hands, finding the strength inside her to be close to him without giving in. She believed him. He'd always had a sincerity about him that a lot of guys she met didn't have. But that didn't mean the timing was right. She placed one of her hands in his, remembering how callused they were, how they enveloped hers.

"Thank you. For the apology. Obviously you broke my trust, and I don't know what you're hoping for with this meeting. You... You hurt me, Gideon." She gave his hand a squeeze, knowing some of the issue was her own expectations of him. Dealing with her alcoholic mom all her life, Ella knew he was sick. The girl she'd been a year ago had hoped she'd be enough to change him. The woman she was now knew it was his responsibility to want that change for himself. The past year had brought her a lot of soul-searching, a lot of late night talks with her girlfriends, and a lot of forgiveness.

He held her hand in both of his, running his thumbs over her knuckles.

"I just wanted to see you, Ella. To tell you where

I've been and that I'm sorry. I don't expect anything from you."

She squeezed his hand, nodding while processing what he said. Last time, he'd begged for her to come back to him. Now he knew the consequences of his actions, knew it was futile to beg again.

"I appreciate that," she said, meeting his eyes. His brow had furrowed, his eyes more dim than when they'd started. She knew what it felt like to lose a light in her life, and she hoped he'd find, within himself, the light he'd lost. "Gideon... Where do you want to go from here?"

The words felt out; Ella didn't know what made her ask about their future. She wanted to chalk it up to the next step in this meeting, the way she'd handle any business meeting. She wanted to chalk it up to being so over him, it didn't matter what he said. She wanted to chalk it up to wanting closure so they could move on and never speak to each other again.

But she knew those were all lies. She knew the pull in her heart had never left. She knew that, if she was honest with herself, sitting across from him now had only reignited the fire he'd left behind.

11

Where do you want to go from here?

Those were the last words Gideon had expected to come out of her mouth.

He sat a little straighter, contemplating his response. He knew he'd hurt her, broken her trust. Caused irreparable damage. Why didn't she just walk away? The flutter in his belly was dangerous. It was not okay to get his hopes up, even if his heart had other plans.

He released her hand, busying himself with his cooling tea. She did the same, but her eyes never left his face while she let him have this moment. They set their cups down at the same time. She laughed and he smiled at the sound.

"I guess sometimes we have good timing, eh?" His remark caused her to laugh more.

"If only we could be more consistent, right?" She cleared her throat, eyes sparkling while she regarded him. "Just tell me the truth, Gideon. What do you want?"

"I want you. I've always only wanted you."

The words made their place at the table, sitting between them in the silence that followed.

"What do you want, Ella?"

She sighed, leaned back in her chair.

"Honestly? I want you, too. But really, I want to be your friend first," she said. "We're both different people from last year. I want to know you, and I want you to know me." She shifted in her seat, breaking eye contact and folding her arms across her chest. "Besides, I'm pretty sure AA has a rule about relationships."

Shit.

In his excitement to just be near her, he'd forgotten. Even if she wanted to be with him, he couldn't be with her. Not if he wanted to be serious about himself. AA wasn't about her. It wasn't for her. He needed to be on this path for himself.

"Will we even be able to just be friends, Ella?"

She pursed her lips. "No idea. It's worth a shot though, right?" She rested her chin in her hand.

"Always." He raised his cup between them. "Cheers, to relearning one another."

"Cheers." She clinked her glass against his, and they took sips of the lukewarm tea before settling into silence. Not awkward, rather an easy state of being Gideon had always felt with her. Her fingers played with the rim of her cup.

"Tell me about your business." He refilled their cups with warm tea left in the pot. He wanted to hear her voice as often as possible, especially if she was open to being friends. He'd find a way to fill the Ella-shaped hole in his heart, and he'd find a way to put together the pieces of her heart he was responsible for breaking.

She sat up and smiled, a slight blush creeping across her cheeks. This was the Ella he remembered; it was a sweet contrast to the powerful woman she now embodied. "It's really good. Like, really really good. We work out of a co-working space and are on the verge of signing a really big client," she said. "Actually, when you came to visit me in the office, that was who I was on the phone with." Her eyes met his, clouded over with something he couldn't place. *Disappointment? Hurt?*

Gideon felt heavy, and he wondered if they could ever move past the weight of their history. "I'm sorry, that wasn't my smartest move, to show up at your place of work. Did the call go okay?"

"Um, I mean I think so, but you definitely interrupted," she said, sighing. "It's okay, just... please don't do that again. Not while we're figuring this out. Us out."

He nodded. "Of course, I understand. We need some space but hopefully not too much. You know I need to make fun of you turning every head when you laugh." He smiled, hoping he could lighten things enough for her to start opening up to him again.

She laughed. "You always did think that was funny."

"More like a superpower, commanding all the attention in the room."

"It's not like you don't do the same when you walk in, all broad shoulders and blue eyes."

He felt the heat surge through his body and couldn't stop his dick from responding. Especially when she stared at him like that, lips moist from the tea. "Ella... If we're going to try this friend thing, we probably shouldn't be talking about... physical stuff. You know I can go on about you all day." All he wanted was to kiss her skin. To flip her around, lift up her dress around those wide hips, and sink so deep into her until all she could think about was him. Maybe bite her shoulder, spank that sweet ass. Remind her how much he was still hers, and that she was still his. He cleared his throat, shifting in his seat to make his hard-on more comfortable.

"You're right, I'm sorry." She licked her lips. "I guess friends is going to be harder than I thought."

12

Well, that didn't go how she'd planned.

Sure, Ella wanted to be friends with her super hot ex-boyfriend. But more than that she wanted him to pull her hair while he thrust into her, help her forget everything bad that had happened between them. Being with him was as easy as she'd remembered, and she'd let her thoughts get carried away. And then her mouth. They'd laughed it off and stayed another hour before she had to head home to finish some work, but she'd felt the heat flowing off him. He clearly wanted to take her as bad as she needed him to.

She groaned, resting her head on the desk in her apartment. Trying to concentrate on work when Gideon was on her mind was never easy. It didn't help that he looked better than ever. She'd seen the changes a program like AA could make. Her mom always came home from rehab less bloated, eyes clear, and with a drive to live her life like never before. It didn't always last long, but Ella had always loved seeing that woman. The one she could only get glimpses of in her early movies. Speaking of which, she needed to plan a visit to see her mom in rehab. Her mind tumbled in that direction but a meow hailing from her feet broke her from the planning. Pollack wrapped himself around her legs, each meow more eager than the last in an attempt to get his dinner. She picked him up on her way to the small kitchen. He sank into her and she whispered sweet nothings to him before obliging his request.

Metallic-y salmon filled the air and she tried not to gag. She'd do anything for her fur baby but the wet food always made her second-guess her choice in a partner. She remembered how Gideon knew his way around the kitchen, and her mouth salivated at the memories of his cooking. And his shirtless chest flexing with every turn of the spatula or slice of the garlic bread.

"Ugh, Pollack, what am I going to do?" She watched him lick his bowl clean while she contemplated what food to order in. Now that the business with Rachel was taking off and she still worked a couple shifts at The Lava Java, Ella worked less hours and had more money. She liked the feeling of abundance, so while she didn't need the barista job, she held onto it to build up her safety net for when they moved the publicity business to the Big Apple. It also enabled her love for takeout. She placed the order for Mexican and decided what background show she could put on while she took care of some busy work.

She settled on an old comedy favorite, her phone interrupting the punchline.

"Hello?" Ella asked.

"Hey Ella, do you have a moment?" Rachel's voice cut through the noise. Ella froze. She thought the Mexican restaurant had called back with a question and she hadn't expected the stern tone of her business partner.

"Oh, um, yeah. Of course. What's up?" She paused the show, anxiety creeping up her throat.

"I was debating when and how to bring this up, but a couple days ago I received an email from Charlie at that small publishing house, Blue Bird Books. The one you had a phone call with when Gideon interrupted."

Damnit. "Oh, really? Is everything okay?"

"Not really, Ella. She said she felt you were really distracted, including not keeping up with the conversation and saying you sent over different documents than the ones she needs. She was concerned about moving forward if that's how we usually operate. She's still unsure and wants more time to think on it. Obviously I smoothed things over as best I could, but it's been bothering me. I wanted to start the week with this out of the way."

"Oh my god, I'm so sorry, Rachel." Ella curled up on her comfy purple couch, sinking into the corner. Wanting to disappear. "I dropped some of the papers I needed and they got all jumbled. I thought I ended everything smoothly though. What can I do to help fix this?"

"Honestly, I'm not sure. Have you spoken to Gideon about making sure he doesn't show up at the office again? As friendly as I want us to be and as friendly as we already are, I would also like to keep personal business separate from our professional business."

Pollack hopped up beside her, laying down for belly pets. Ella stroked him absentmindedly. "Yeah, we actually met for tea. I mentioned it, he promised he wouldn't show up. I promise something like that won't happen again. We should have another call with Charlie where we're both there, I think it'll show her we have our shit together and we're a team."

"I suggested the very same thing but she wants to wait until next week." Rachel sighed. "We really need this client if we want to move to New York City. I know there's nothing we can really do right now, I'm just a little upset."

Ella pulled Pollack into her lap. "I'm getting takeout and will probably watch a movie while working, do you wanna come over?"

"No, it's okay. Thank you. I have this super fancy dinner my dad needs me to attend. It'll be okay, I'm sure of it. I'll see you tomorrow, right?"

"Absolutely, Rachel. Have fun tonight and if there's anything I can do, please let me know." They hung up as the delivery guy's call came through.

Ella ran down the steps to collect the food, thankful her noisy neighbors and their barking dog had moved out a few months prior. She heaved the food meant for two or three people up the worn steps, replaying the conversation with Rachel while she plated her meal. Ella settled back on the sofa, her faithful companion at her side, all drive to work having gone out the window. She sighed. At least the possibility of losing a new client helped distract her from wanting to be with a man she loved but who wasn't ready for her.

13

Gideon always forgot how small the rehearsal room felt. The three other band members and Tom were all over six feet tall and took up so much space. He was still learning the ways alcohol had numbed him and spatial awareness seemed to be one of them. Tom had added fancy bottled soda to the fridge alongside the beer and Gideon wondered how easy it'd be to "accidentally" grab a beer instead of the nonalcoholic option.

"Yo man, is this about Ella?" Anthony's voice cut through his silent wishes. Gideon had dropped new lyrics on the folding table for them to review when he'd walked in and taken his usual place by the window. And the fridge.

Gideon looked at his bandmate, his cousin. "Yeah, we met up the other day." The man who, over a year ago, had convinced Gideon to drink even though he'd promised Ella he wouldn't.

"That's good, we always liked her." Anthony took a swig from a beer bottle.

"I can tell. This song is another single and belongs on the album, near *Halo*," Tom piped in. Lucas and Ryan were going over bass lines and drum rhythms in the back.

"Gid, how do you feel this one playing out?" Ryan looked up from his bass, fingering the strings.

"Um, definitely acoustic but I know we need a radio hit." Gideon lifted off the sill and picked up his electric guitar. "How's this?"

The instrument felt at home in his hands. Like Ella. He closed his eyes, strumming the notes he'd heard in his head when he wrote the lyrics in his apartment. So far music was the only time he didn't miss alcohol, but it made him miss her more than ever. His voice rang through the room. He'd worked a lot on forgiveness over the past few months, and Ella had greeted him with the same. He knew the situation was delicate. He also knew it was as close to a second chance as he was going to get, and the new song spoke to the dreams and gratitude in his heart.

When he finished, he opened his eyes and

looked around the room. The guys stood in a circle around him, nodding their heads.

"Goddamn. It's good to have you back, man," Lucas said, sitting behind his drum kit, tapping the beat on the bass drum.

Anthony stood behind the keyboard, setting his half-empty bottle on the ground. "What're we feeling, Pops?" He directed the question at Tom. "Synth or grand?"

"Let's see... *Halo* has synth. *Flask* also has synth and *Let Go* is acoustic. Let's try piano for this one and see what happens. We could also try sax or strings."

The band settled in while Tom leaned against the folding table. Lucas tapped out the beat while Gideon repeated the first few bars of the song so Ryan and Anthony could figure out their parts. They played through the song once.

"How about we start with a sax solo and then move into the beat? We can reprise it before each chorus?" Tom suggested.

Anthony fixed the settings on the keyboard, playing the jazzy sax notes until it fit the tone of the other instruments. Tom nodded his head. "Okay, great. Let's try it. Lucas, could you quit the cymbals and quiet the snare?"

The sax started them off and, after a couple bars,

the rest of the guys jumped in. They cut out before the first chorus, allowing the keyboard sax loop to play solo after the drop. They picked up where they left off for the chorus, building to the verse and dropping again before the second chorus. Tom clapped as the finished the song.

"Eternal Youths is back! Nicely done guys." He picked up a lyric sheet. "Based off the sound and lyrics, I say this should be at the end. It's a good ramp up for the second album. What do you think?"

The band put in their agreements before commiserating on changing some of the instrumentals. Anthony polished off his beer and grabbed another, flashing Gideon a smile. It reminded him of old times, of the clink of bottles, of overlapping cheers. Now that Ella was back in the picture, he felt more whole than he'd ever felt before. And he didn't want to be numb to that feeling ever again.

14

The week was moving particularly slow. Especially given the last minute coffee meet-up Ella had made with Gideon for today. Waiting to hear back from Charlie at Blue Bird Books didn't help, but Rachel seemed confident everything would work out after she'd let out steam on their phone call.

Ella leaned back in her chair, looking around the small office. Rachel had brought in some new plants Monday morning that brightened the space. They each now had a small succulent on their desks, some sort of larger majestic palm plant by the side table next to the loveseat, and a hanging fern in one of the corners by a window. She stretched, her bare feet running through the short carpet, sheath dress pulling against her hips. She stood, shuffled some of the papers on her desk into a neat pile for the next day, and slipped on her heels. Rachel had left early and Ella was thankful for the time to compose herself before meeting Gideon. They'd been texting nonstop since they'd met for tea. She couldn't help herself. Anytime her phone buzzed, her hands always shook. Her breath always caught, her skin always flushed. She'd reach for the device that held her heart, hoping his name would flash across her screen.

She locked the office behind her, heading to the communal restroom while checking her phone for the millionth time but knowing he wouldn't respond to her, "See you soon!" text. Ella didn't know what made her revert to feeling sixteen, crushing on the first boy that paid her any real attention. She thought she'd left that person behind. But of course, leave it to the tall, brooding, tattooed man that was Gideon to bring it out of her. Ella checked herself in the full-length mirror, smoothing her dress and reapplying her lipstick. Julie had always been great with hair and makeup and had helped Ella find her mid-20's glow-up. Her blonde hair was sleek and lightly blow-dried, creating a small wave that finished off her polished professional look. She slipped on her leather jacket, a thrift store find that fit perfectly, as she made her way to where she was meeting Gideon.

Frosting sat at the top of Main Street, the last reprieve before Main Street turned into a highway. Made famous by it's overly sweet confections, it doubled as a cozy coffee shop and was a nice change of pace from The Lava Java, which stood in the center of Main Street. The short walk from the office was made difficult by her heels, and Ella burst through the door panting. She didn't need to look around. The blue-black of Gideon's hair stood out against the white walls, and he was staring right at her with the sexy smirk that almost never seemed to leave his face. At least when he was looking at her. She made her way over to him, the click of her heels on the tile boosting her confidence, even if they did nothing for the wetness blossoming between her thighs.

"Hey, there," Ella said as she sat across from him. "Sorry I'm a little late, I had some things I needed to wrap up at the office." She took a deep breath, slowly letting it out while she took him in. The slope of his broad shoulders, the tattoos she'd traced many times trailing from large biceps to skilled fingers. She swallowed, pushing down the urge to straddle him.

He leaned forward, some of his hair falling into

his eyes. "No worries, I didn't know what you wanted so I waited to order. You look nice, I like the jacket," he said, fingering her sleeve. "It's different."

She met his piercing gaze, his eyes reflecting the sunlight streaming through the window and turning them a bright sky blue. "I wanted to try something new."

"Me, too."

Her breath hitched at the implication. They were both different, both seeking something they'd been missing.

"Gideon..."

15

He sighed, standing and placing his hands in his pockets. "I know. What will the lady have to order?"

Gideon couldn't help himself. He wanted her. He missed her. He loved her. He'd never stopped loving her. Staring at her now, delicate face upturned, hair burning in the golden light... He fell for her all over again.

"Um, I'll just have a black coffee," Ella said.

He cracked a smile. "No treat? Maggie seemed upset and I must say, it's unlike you to not want dessert."

That brought a belly laugh from her lips. "I don't need it," she said as she stood to join him. Her body was almost flush against his, and he had to stop himself from pulling her into his arms.

"Nobody said anything about need."

His face was close enough to kiss hers, to meld their bodies into one. He remembered the feel of her in his hands, the way her curves overflowed and filled him. She gazed up at him, her eyes soft in the shadow of him, bow lips parted.

"Gideon... This is hard enough without... implications."

Her dress hid her chest but he could feel her heart racing between them. He raised his hand to her cheek, stroking the flushed skin with the pad of his thumb.

"It's hard for me too, Ella. I'm sorry, I just... I miss you."

She sighed, closing her eyes and leaning into his palm.

"I miss you, too." She opened her eyes and moved past him. "But we can't think on that. We deserve something different and owe it to ourselves to find that, no matter the form it comes in."

She stood in the short line, her back to him. That dress did wonders for her figure, highlighting her narrow waist and wide hips, her heels lengthening the strong legs he'd always loved. He walked to her and stood with his chest to her back. Resting chin on her shoulder, he wrapped his arms around her waist. Held her close against him, breathed her in. She leaned back, accepting the space he'd always saved for her. The place she belonged. They both knew it.

"Okay, fine. I'll have a peanut butter chocolate cupcake. And a black coffee. But you got the tea, so let me get this one." She pulled away from him and moved to the register without glancing back.

"As you wish."

That got her. Ella turned around, the corners of her beautiful mouth lifting slightly.

"Oh, you're smooth." She shook her head but the smile stayed. "What will you have?"

"A black coffee and a vanilla cupcake, please."

She placed the order with the cashier and Gideon took their coffees from the second server behind the counter. He carried them to where they'd been sitting, setting the large mugs on the coffee table as Ella placed the delicacies beside them. They settled on the couch. Close enough to touch, to lean in and fall, but knowing if they crossed that line there'd be no going back.

The comfortable silence fell between them as Ella dug into her cupcake and Gideon tried to think of something to talk about. Over tea, they'd caught up on the surface details. Work, tour, work, band, work.

Might as well jump in.

"How's your mom, Ella?"

The question visibly threw her. She shifted to face him.

"She's... good," she said through a mouthful of peanut butter and chocolate. "She's actually in rehab right now."

"That's good."

Ella went back to her cupcake, slower than before, while Gideon watched her. The silence was borderline awkward, a feeling they rarely experienced.

"You know, you can tell me more, Ella. You can be open with me."

Taking a moment to think, Ella swallowed her bite with coffee. "I know, Gideon. I just don't really know how anymore. And what a question to lead with." She chuckled, fingered the handle of her mug.

He nodded, smiling a little. He knew if he wanted her to be vulnerable, he'd have to return the favor.

"You know me, I never beat around the bush." He started in on his cupcake. "My sponsor told me to consider rehab if the program didn't work, but honestly I feel pretty good most of the time." He felt her gaze on him but stayed busy licking the frosting off the little cake. Wishing he was licking it off her skin.

"I'm really glad you're finding your footing, Gideon. I'm sure the past few months have been an adjustment."

He nodded, not returning her stare. He felt the heat from her body as she shifted closer to him, placing her arm around him, her cheek on his shoulder.

A hug. A stepping stone. A new beginning.

16

He smelled just as she remembered. A little spicy, a little sweet. A perfect combination of man. His shoulder fit perfectly in the hollow of her cheek and she remembered why she couldn't stay away.

Ella didn't know why she gave into touching him, holding him, but she didn't stop herself. Gideon held still. It seemed as though he was barely breathing, trying to see if the moment was real.

"Ya know, I know how this works," Ella said. "I've been through it with my mom. You can always talk to me. She was supposed to get out for the millionth time a couple months ago but we talked it over and she felt she needed more time. I get it." She thought back to her last visit with her mom. The stark room contrasting with the healthy flush in Margaret's cheeks. She'd been in sixty days already, but Ella had seen the fear hidden in her eyes at the thought of coming home. Of having to be an actress and a mom, to make money and pay bills and take care of herself. Ella had seen that look before. It was the look where, at the tender age of fourteen, Ella had to learn the difference between Mom and Margaret. For her own sake.

She rubbed her hand along Gideon's bicep, turning to look at him.

"It has been an adjustment." He nodded, staring at their mess on the table. "But even when it's hard, like when I'm with the band, I feel so good and I can remind myself of all the times I felt so bad or did stupid things. And it's enough." He turned to look at her. Their noses almost touched and she smiled at the thought of an eskimo kiss.

"What's that look for, beautiful?" He smiled back.

It felt like old times, like nothing had changed. Except Ella knew that everything had. He'd taken the step, alone, to change.

"Gideon, you have to be careful with words like that."

"You know, there's no real rule about relationships. It's more a suggestion," he said as his fingers traced her knee. Shivers ran down her spine. The touch reminded her of the nights they spent together, the shapes they made beneath the covers. The way he moved between her thighs with his tongue, fingers, and beautiful cock. Ella swallowed and shifted her body towards his. Tried to fight the heat rising in her belly.

"I know, but I also want to be smart about this. If we have anything left, I don't want to ruin it by moving too fast." She brushed a stray lock out of his eyes and rested her hand on his neck.

"What if being smart is picking up where we left off and relearning each other?" His eyes pierced hers, the deep blue an ocean she longed to drown in.

Ella let his words hang between them, binding them to what they'd lost and what they hoped for. She'd give anything to have him hold her again. But she also knew from past experience people weren't always ready when they thought they were. She said as much, never releasing her hand from his warm skin.

"People on all paths say they're ready but no one really knows until they're in it. What are you scared of?" He kept his gaze on her, brow furrowing.

She felt like Gideon stole all the air out of the room. Everything felt tight and close while she tried to come up with an answer. Where to start?

Leave.

She had to get out before she caved. Before she burst into tears over the realization she had hidden her feelings behind work. That she had as many walls as he had.

17

Gideon hurried to catch up to Ella.

What the fuck.

She'd just popped up, said she had to leave, and took off. He'd tried calling after her, asking what was wrong, but she didn't respond. He saw her walking as fast as those high heels would let her down the hill. He sighed and, thankful for his long legs, caught up fairly quickly. He stopped in front of her, holding her shoulders in his hands. She wouldn't look at him, but what he saw broke his heart.

She was crying.

The droplets stained her dress, the rivulets over her lip trembling.

"Okay, Ella, it's okay," he said, pulling her against his chest. Gideon hated seeing anyone cry, but the fact it was her broke his heart. He replayed the conversation in his mind and couldn't see what he'd done wrong. He held her on the sidewalk, hiding her from the rolling cars and sidewalk passersby. He knew she had her own demons but he would protect her from what he could.

"Hey, I drove here. Let me drive you home," he murmured in her ear. She squeezed him tighter and he rubbed his hand along her back. "C'mon, darlin'." He slowly released her from his embrace, leaving his hand on her lower back to guide her to his car parked behind Frosting. He was glad for the twilight hiding them from public eye, especially once in the safety of the car. Ella hadn't spoken since she'd left the building in a flurry, but he remembered where she lived and drove them in silence.

Gideon pulled in front of the yoga studio that stood as the base for her apartment building. He turned the car off and faced her.

"Okay, Ella. Forgive me for crossing any lines here, but I don't feel comfortable leaving you alone in this state." She didn't move, just sat in the seat looking at her hands. "I'd like to come upstairs with you. We can sit in silence or watch TV or you can tell me what's on your mind."

"Okay." Her voice was barely audible, but it was enough for him. He got out and opened the passenger side, shutting the door after she stepped out. The front door to Ella's building was as unlocked and sticky as it'd been the last time he'd been here, and he watched her struggle with the knob before it gave way. They climbed the worn steps, each creak a footnote in their story. Her hips swayed with ever slow step she took, reminding him of how they moved above him. He tried to keep his eyes on her legs, to focus on being the rock she clearly needed, but the curve of her calf and the memory of how it tasted when he'd kissed them was a memory that haunted him. It only brought him back to being wrapped around her.

They reached the door to her apartment slower than two flights of stairs usually amounted to. She unlocked the door, kicked off her heels, and went to the kitchen to fill a couple glasses with water. Gideon looked around. Her place hadn't changed at all. Floral armchair, purple couch, books, pictures. He circled the small space, the warm smell of her everywhere.

"Here," Ella said, handing him one of the glasses. "I'm going to change real quick." She took off down the short hall to her bedroom. He took a sip, settling on the couch while he waited. When she returned, he couldn't help but smile. Her dark grey sweatpants had large blossoming flowers all over them, her pink cotton shirt hugging every curve. She pulled the long sleeves to cover her hands and gave him a small smile.

"You look cozy. Come here." He scooted over, opening the side of his body for her to crawl into. His angel needed to be comforted, to be held. And by God, he was going to be the one to hold her. She hesitated before sighing and curling into him. She fit like she always had. Like she belonged there.

They sat in silence, which was just fine by Gideon. He relished the feel of her against him, drank in the whiff of vanilla and sandalwood anytime she shifted. He never thought he'd be in this position again, and he was going to enjoy it as long as he could.

18

"I'm sorry." The words just came out of her mouth, and Ella wasn't even sure what she was sorry for.

He squeezed her shoulder, pulling her closer to him, kissing the top of her head. "You have nothing to be sorry for."

She chewed her lower lip. He had been her friend in the past, and he could be again. If she let him. "I just... I don't know what happened. I got really sad and needed to leave."

"I get that. You're not the first person to get hit with a wave of emotion and feel like the walls were caving in." He paused. Ella looked up at him, meeting his gaze. "What made you sad, darlin'?"

She looked away and became overly fascinated with a loose string on the hem of her sleeve. She didn't know how to tell him they were more alike than she'd wanted to believe, that she was terrified of getting close to someone and accidentally giving them power over her heart. That she'd already done that with him and missed him more than anything.

"Ella, our walls are only as high as we allow them to be. How about you tell me something you're scared of or sad about and I'll tell you one of mine?" His voice cut through her thoughts, cut through the noise, and brought her back to just her and him.

"Okay." She took a deep breath. "I'm scared that I'll never be able to be close to someone. Not as much as I want to be."

"I'm scared I only know how to fuck things up, especially when they're good."

"I'm scared that if I trust you, every time you're on tour I'll lose you again." She looked at him, took in the only man she ever wanted to love. Pain was written all over his face and she adjusted so her body faced his.

"I'm sad that I hurt you so much and I don't know how to fix it." Gideon's admission matched the words in her heart.

"I'm just... sad. I'm sad that my mom struggles so much and I'm sad that you do, too. I'm sad that I've built so many walls but refuse to acknowledge them. I'm sad I felt like I was better and stronger and... I'm not." Ella felt her voice start to break. Finally letting out her pent-up emotions felt really good. Really, really good. "I'm sad that I hinged so much of myself on whether I was enough for you. I'm sad that I ever loved you as much as I did. And while I've unhinged my happiness from my expectations, I'm even more sad that I never stopped loving you. I'm sad that you're the one I want. Always."

The verbal floodgates had opened and she ended her word vomit with a heavy breath. Her face was wet, and she wiped the few leaked tears before wrapping her arms around herself, replacing the weight that had lifted with her many admissions. She couldn't remember the last time she'd been that open and honest with anyone. The relief outweighed the fear, the anxiety, of what would come next.

They sat in silence.

"Your turn," she said, chuckling.

Gideon smiled in return. "Yeah, no kidding. Do you feel better?" His hand reached for hers, enveloping it in warmth. Safety.

"Yeah, I do actually." She squeezed his hand. "I didn't realize how much was... there. But it is your turn. You're not getting out of this that easily."

He nodded. "Honestly, I'm just scared I messed

things up with you. I've always believed in us. No one's ever made me feel the way you do. I know you're scared to try things again and I don't blame you. But like you said, we're different people. I want to show you that."

"But why can't we just be friends?"

"Ella, you know the answer to that."

She did know the answer because it was the same one she had. There was no way she could trust herself to just be friends with the gentle giant before her when all she wanted was to fall asleep beside him. To kiss him good morning, to feel his skin against hers. It was a fruitless venture, and she knew it. With him, it was all or nothing. It always had been.

"I need to hear you tell me," she said.

Gideon leaned in, his face almost against hers. She felt the tickle of his breath as he shared the moments she wanted. The experiences he wanted to have with her, the way he wanted to touch her. How he wanted to make her laugh. He whispered these truths, and they answered the call in her heart. She couldn't stop herself when she interrupted his monologue with a kiss. Her hands found his face, his neck, his hair, remembered every curve and pulse.

She was home.

19

As surprised as he'd been when she kissed him, that didn't stop Gideon from deep-diving into it. Her hands graced his skin, tangled in his hair, and he pulled her closer. This was better than any memory, any dream. She tasted sweeter, more powerful, than before. He wanted so much more.

Their tongues sparred, the heat building between them. He needed to make up for every missed kiss. Every missed moment. He shifted, pulling her on top of him so he was between her thighs. He wanted her to feel in control, although he'd be lying if he said he didn't love having her on top of him. He could feel the wet heat blooming at her core, reaching his hard length through his jeans. He groaned, pulling her as tight against him as he could. She'd never be close enough.

Ella pulled his hair, moving her kisses to his neck, tugging his earlobe with her teeth. His hips bucked up, wanting nothing more than to be inside her. To feel every warm inch of her beautiful body against his. Gideon never felt as full or complete as he did when he was with her. He used to think alcohol was what filled the void in his heart, but now that he was sober, he realized it had always been her. He'd just been too drunk to see that. He'd never want another drink again if it meant having her in his arms.

"Oh, God. I need you, Gideon," she moaned against his neck.

"Say no more, angel."

He gripped her hips, pulled her to him while he stood, never letting her go. Their mouths locked once more, breath mixing with each gasp for air.

"Ooof!" Ella cried when he bumped into the corner of the hall in his rush to get her to bed. "Careful there, stud," she said in between kisses, laughing.

"Who, me or the actual stud?" he said, holding her against the wall while he kissed her chest. That made her laugh, the fullness of it turning into a moan when he freed one breast and started sucking on her nipple, a perfect rosebud hardening against his tongue.

"Gideon... Please fuck me."

Her legs were still wrapped around his hips. They pulled him closer to her core as he freed her other breast, giving equal attention to the second rosebud until her back arched against the wall. He was always thankful in these moments that she wore so many dresses and skirts. He felt her wet pussy through the thin fabric of her panties, pressing against his hard cock as he stumbled the rest of the way to her bedroom. A hanging picture may have fallen victim to their passion on the way but Gideon was too preoccupied with getting Ella naked to really care. She didn't seem bothered by the crash, instead reaching to undo his pants.

He laid her on the bed, his body covering her much smaller one. She writhed beneath him. He knew if they crossed this line, there was no going back. Her hand had been successful, loosening his waistband and slipping into his briefs. The sensation made him hiss, ready to be surrounded by her.

Gideon pulled back. He wanted to take his time enjoying her. She was panting, face flushed, eyes hooded with need.

"You're so beautiful." He stroked her cheek,

taking in the curve of her neck. His chest ached with how much he loved her. How much he would never stop loving her. She was deserving of so much more, but she'd never want for love.

A smile broke across her face. "Thank you."

Her fingers toyed with his waistband as he drank her in. Her golden hair fanned out beneath her, luscious thighs spread wide. He knelt between them, heart thumping at the prospect of tasting her once more. He kissed along her inner thigh while his fingers pulled at her panties, the lacy band sliding off her wide hips so she was bared to him. The smell of her honey made him grow rigid and he had to stop himself from devouring her. He bit her flesh, covering the marks with wet kisses to ease the burn, as he reached her core. Fingers dug into his scalp, urging him closer to heaven.

20

His bites along her thighs made all of Ella's nerves stand on edge. Which were only heightened when he'd cooled the sting with his soft lips. And now he was poised above her opening, making her want to beg for more.

He was so goddamn close to giving Ella the ecstasy she'd been dreaming about for months.

So. God. Damn. Close.

But Ella had already given in far more than she'd planned and now they'd reached a point of no return. She wanted this, wanted him, more than anything. She wanted to believe he had changed, that they could be the people they wanted to be together. He looked at her over her belly, a salacious smile playing at his lips while his hands gripped her hips. He leaned closer, never breaking eye contact with her, and she felt the tip of his tongue run through her slick folds.

Oh, yes.

That may have come out as a contented sigh but she couldn't be sure. This was so much nicer than her vibrating friend. He licked once more, harder this time, and her hips bucked when the tip of his tongue reached her clit. The little bundle of nerves was having a field day with the care and attention this old stranger was giving them. Ella felt the fire in her belly building, the need to fall over the edge coming closer and closer.

She gasped as he added his fingers. He pumped them, slowly, building the blaze inside her. She called out his name, knowing the word on her lips would make him move faster, harder.

Another finger stretched her further as he moved, his tongue matching the rhythm on her sensitive bud. The pressure against her eternal sweet spot only added to the inferno within her. She felt her muscles shake, the rising tide of pleasure building until it washed over her, drowned her beneath Gideon's careful tongue and skilled fingers.

He lapped at her core while she shook, panted, clutched his hair. Pulled him closer to her. Ella opened her eyes, stars sparkling her vision from the ebbing wave of euphoria. She looked at the man who'd caused it, the small kisses along her inner thighs filling her heart to bursting.

"Come here," she whispered, using her grip on his head to ease him up to her. After the way he'd made her feel, the change from force to tenderness, she needed his lips on hers.

Gideon leveled his body over hers. His hard cock brushed against her thigh while he kissed her deeply, slowly. Like if he stopped, she'd disappear.

"I missed you." His words were a throaty whisper against her mouth, words that spoke to the same feeling she felt in her heart. She pushed against him, aching to get closer, knowing they'd never be close enough.

"I missed you, Gideon." She held his face in her hands. "I need you."

He gazed into her eyes. "I need you, too. I'm not going anywhere this time. I promise." He leaned in to kiss her, adjusting so he was between her legs, and reached over to her nightstand drawer.

She laughed. "Oh, you remembered where I keep my condoms? How very slick of you, sir."

He sat up, tearing the wrapper and rolling the sheath down his thick length.

"Of course I remembered. And if you call me 'sir'

again, you better be prepared for what comes next. Miss."

"I'll keep that - ah!" Ella gasped as he plunged into her. She'd forgotten how he filled her, and he pulled out only to take his time sliding back into her depths so she could fit him. Clutching his shoulders, she let the overwhelming sensation take hold of her body. He fit her perfectly, pushing against her barrier just enough to turn the pain into pleasure, making her moan with the sweet time he took pulling out before thrusting back in. She wrapped herself around him even more, partly to stay close to him and partly to keep the force of his movements from pushing her further up the bed.

The sheen of sweat on him mingled with hers. They slid together while he pushed her to the brink, his heavy panting in her ear. Her hands felt their way around his broad shoulders, his strong biceps, his muscular ass, relearning every curve as he dove into her. His cock was getting harder with every swift motion. The thought of him coming inside her was a dream come true and took her even closer to falling.

She felt the waves overtake her, clutched him for dear life while she came against him, crying out his name. He gave one final thrust, his own pleasure overtaking him. Seeking out her mouth, his lips covered her face until they found what they were looking for. Ella felt the depth of his kiss, how he stayed inside her even after he finished. She felt that feeling she'd been missing, the one where she was exactly where she was meant to be.

21

Gideon's arm tingled. Something was on top of it and he opened his eyes to see what it was.

Ella.

He smiled and kissed her forehead, remembering the night before. He would let his limbs fall asleep every night if it meant waking up beside her. He still couldn't believe his luck. She'd let him kiss her. Caress her body, move above her, feel the waves of pleasure all over her. She clung to him now, holding on as if he was leaving soon. It — she — was a literal dream come true, and he pulled her even closer into his chest. She burrowed deeper into him, relieving some of the pressure from his arm.

A phone rang from somewhere on the ground, the haze of post-coital bliss keeping him from grabbing it. He didn't want this moment to end. It rang again and Gideon realized the ring was from Tom. He pulled Ella tighter, pretending the noise was imaginary. He looked down at her, her shoulders shaking, and pulled back. She was laughing quietly and flashed him a lazy smile.

"Thanks, I couldn't breathe too well down there." She kissed his chest, adjusting so her head rested in the divot between his shoulder and his pec. The dip her head fit perfectly in.

The phone rang again and he sighed.

"Do you have to get that?" Her voice was small, lost somewhere between the ring of the phone and thoughts of what would happen once this moment ended. What would happen between them once they acknowledged the real-world consequences of their night together.

"Yeah, unfortunately. It's Tom," he said, kissing her forehead once more before sitting up. The space she'd been in was cold, and he ached to return to their little bubble. He found the phone in his discarded jeans, thankfully close to the bed, and he brought it back under the covers with him. Ella took the place she'd left.

Tom had left a voicemail after the last call. Last-minute band practice Gideon was apparently late for. Booked recording time on Monday for the new song at the end of the album. And to call him back immediately.

"Is everything okay?" Ella asked.

"Yeah. Band practice, apparently. Guess I forgot. I'm sorry, darlin', I wanted to make you breakfast."

Shit.

Gideon realized he'd missed a meeting last night. He'd gone to at least one AA meeting every week since he returned from tour. Missing something that had been imperative to his health for weeks was weird to think about. But it was even weirder to think how he hadn't even realized he'd missed it. He hadn't even thought of a drink since before their coffee meet-up, when he missed the familiar warmth of liquid courage.

"Aw, man. They don't need you, right?" Her face pulled him back to the bed. She started kissing his chest but never venturing too far from her horizontal position. Gideon turned to face her, shelving his thoughts on making the next meeting. Another problem for another time. He scooted down so they were nose to nose, the covers pulled up to their chins. Comfy. Just the way he liked it.

"I mean, I'm not the lead guitarist or anything. I think they'll manage," he whispered, his fingers stroking the hair from her forehead.

"Great, then I'll take you up on breakfast." She pressed her lips against his, holding them there while she pushed herself even closer. Gideon felt the words she couldn't say, his tongue breaking through the barrier in an attempt to silently share his own. He needed her. Her light, love, trust. The way she touched him, kissed him, held him. He wanted to sink deeper into her until they were one, until they could never be separated again.

"Goddamn it." He tore himself away from her at the sound of his phone ringing. Again. He'd managed to push her onto her back, his bare chest pressed against hers as he slowly pulled moans from those sweet lips of hers. The band of her lacy panties was held between his fingers, ready to be stripped away.

"Maybe it'll go away?" she whispered against his lips, her own hands having found their way to the length of his cock held prisoner by his briefs. He could hardly think straight with all the blood rushing to the wrong head.

The ring started again after a slight pause. He hung his head, closing his eyes and breathing her in. If he had to leave the heaven they'd carved out, he'd take every memory he could with him. Her hand ran along his back, sending shivers down his spine.

"Guess I'll have to take a rain check." She shifted so her legs tangled with his.

"You doing this isn't making this any easier."

"That's the point." She kissed him again, harder, biting his lip and tugging. Ignoring the phone, asking him to stay.

"Ella, I really do have to go. I'm sorry." Breathing was difficult when she moved against him like that. She'd spread her legs, pulled him closer until he was between them. His hard cock rested on her damp panties, her opening just beyond reach. If they weren't in the way, he could just slide right...

Fucking relentless. The phone was going off again.

"Fine, get your phone." She tried to throw her head back, exasperated, but the tight quarters didn't do her any favors.

"You know I'd rather get you even wetter," he murmured against her neck, giving the sensitive area of her exposed neck a kiss before reaching for the phone on the nightstand. Ryan had called and so had Anthony. He was apparently very late and he wanted to chew them out for taking him away from the one thing that mattered most to him.

22

She felt like she was perpetually wet. Or horny. Or both.

At least since Gideon had come back into the picture.

She clenched her thighs at the thought of him the other night, how he'd filled the space that had been there since he'd left on tour. She'd forgotten how full his cock felt inside her, how slow he'd had to go at first so she could fit him. The way his hips settled between her thighs, each thrust drawing them closer than the last.

"Hey, Ella?"

She looked up at her business partner, the vivid memory dissipating as she realized Rachel had spoken to her.

"Sorry, what was that?" Ella adjusted in her desk

chair, smoothing her french blue sheath dress and trying to ignore the heat between her legs.

"I was saying how I need you to focus. I spoke to Charlie, from Blue Bird Books? She wants to schedule a call with both of us on the line."

Right. Charlie had wanted time to look over their contract and proposal, especially after she felt Ella had been a space case on the call. And she wasn't wrong, thanks to Gideon walking through the door after over a year of being gone.

"Oh, good. Do you think she'll sign with us?" Ella shuffled the papers on her desk, finding the copies of what she'd sent over.

"Honestly, I don't know. Will you be able to maintain a conversation with us if you're on the call?"

Ella looked up to see Rachel staring her down, leaning against her desk with arms crossed. Rachel was generally a warm person but didn't hesitate to put others in line. The ice in her voice, although not unusual, was directed at Ella and she felt herself stiffen.

"Yes. I'm sorry, Rachel. It was a one-time thing, a unique situation. I already apologized and said it won't happen again."

Rachel's face turned stony, peeling herself off her post and walking behind her desk.

"And I appreciate that, but this is a huge account. I've had a real estate agent looking at office locations in New York City. We need to take ourselves seriously if we expect clients to. You didn't do that, and even today, just now, when I was speaking you were zoned out. That's not what I signed up for when we partnered up." She pulled out an old-school leather planner from her drawer. "Are you available, and I do mean available, later this week?"

Ella opened her Google Calendar on the computer, trying not to be phased by Rachel's attitude. She took a deep breath, her fingers sore from the nail biting she'd been doing lately. They were partners, Ella wasn't a child or an employee, but she was also in the wrong. Blue Bird Books was a perfect opportunity to show Rachel she was serious about their business while also commanding respect as an equal.

"Yes, I can be available whenever you need me. While I understand where you're coming from, we're in this together." She looked at Rachel. "We're both used to being our own boss and telling people what to do. We need to navigate working together from a place of respect, for our work but most importantly for each other."

Rachel put her pen down and chewed the inside of her lip. A long silence followed as they regarded one another.

"I'm sorry," Rachel sighed, relaxing against her chair. "You're right. Does next Monday afternoon work, say 1 p.m.?"

That was the best response Ella could hope for from her partner. "Yeah, that works fine."

Silence ensued, tense but slowly dissipating.

"So... Speaking of being distracted, how's Gideon? I need deets, you know it's like the desert over here," Rachel said, writing in her planner.

Liking to keep a written and an electronic record of their meetings, Ella sent over a Google Calendar invite for the meeting to delay going into those sordid details.

"You know, me and Julie have been doing a biweekly girl's night since college. You should come to the next one. There will be plenty of dirty deets to go around." She looked at her partner, knowing it was past time they truly became friends. Maybe Ella could figure out why Rachel bounced between hot and cold so often.

Rachel looked at her, a smile slowly working its way across her face.

"Really? That sounds so fun. I'd really like that. Thank you, Ella."

"Sure thing. The more the merrier, right?" She smiled back. "In any case, tell me more about this real estate agent and their findings. I didn't realize you'd already been looking into moving."

23

The recording studio was spacious, holding a variety of instruments and the members of Eternal Youths with plenty of room for dancing. Or pacing, as Gideon did in between every take.

Tom was on the other side of the glass, talking to the producers and Nate, their label rep. Gideon felt the carpet beneath his feet while he tried to burn off some of the excess adrenaline from working on their first studio album. Energy he would've rather spent on pleasing Ella.

"Gid, you're making me dizzy," Anthony said, sipping his beer.

"Seriously, man," Lucas chimed in, tapping his bass drum. "Can we try to figure out the sax part since that song's ending the album and we need a good finish?"

"I think we should figure out a title first since we'll need the boss's input on the music," Ryan said, running a hand through his short hair.

The guys nodded in agreement and started throwing out one- or two-word title ideas, keeping the style in line with the other songs on the album. Gideon listened to the guys, thinking about the most recent song Ella had inspired. Ever since they'd met she'd always been his angel, his goddess, and he had wanted this song to pay tribute to her grace.

"Divinity." He stopped pacing. The word embodied her and fit with the rest of the songs on the album.

The guys looked at one another, nodding while they thought it over.

"I say let's keep it as a working title for now, but it does fit with the others so we could keep it," Ryan said. "We go from *Flask* to *Divinity* and set up nicely for the next album. And I also think it works with the growth of the band and with you, Gideon."

Gideon broke eye contact, the reference to his recovery causing him to walk stiffly to the stand where his guitar rested as Tom's voice came over the speaker.

"You guys ready to rock? We want to run through it one more time like before and then the studio sax player will be here in the next half hour or so." Tom clicked off to ask the producer and Nate something before returning to the band. "We can finalize the sound with him and record the album, which Nate can pass off to the press as an exclusive sneak peak."

The guys settled into their instruments, running through the song like they had played back in their rehearsal space. They made a few tweaks before the studio sax, Max, showed up. They hadn't been told anything about him, and Gideon was pleasantly surprised by the warmth emanating from him as he shook everyone's hand. His smile took up his whole face, and he tied his dreads up before slinging his alto sax around his neck.

"Alright, catch me up. You're the word slinger, ya?" His dark eyes burned into Gideon, catching him off guard.

"Um, yeah. But we all worked on the instrumentals." Gideon took in Max's navy cardigan and torn gray jeans. Max was his height, even with his shoulders relaxed.

"I get that, but the word slinger has the soul of the song. The sax brings the soul to the instrumentals. I need the lyrics in order to do that." Max smiled, fingering his instrument and turning to the group. "Run through it for me once, guys. Then I want the nutshell lowdown on the lyrics so I can make my adjustments."

The guys looked at one another before jumping into the song. Max closed his eyes, nodding to the beat of Lucas's bass and snare. Gideon closed his eyes while he sang, picturing the body, the woman, he worshipped.

"Mm, yeah." Max's voice came in at the quick, quiet taps on the cymbals as Gideon dove into the second verse. Gideon opened his eyes, watching Max bop along to the song. They crescendoed into the final chorus and slowed down for the outro.

"Damn, that is a sexy song." Max opened his eyes, looking at each of the guys in turn. "I felt that in my bones." He dramatically clutched his chest, dissipating some of the nervous energy they felt at integrating a new member. He settled on Gideon, waiting for the explanation on the lyrics.

"Um, well..." Gideon strummed his guitar, trying to buy himself time. How could he explain Ella and the way she made him feel to someone who hadn't even met her?

"Man, I know it's about a girl," Max said. "Sounds like she's special, you fucked up, and she's giving you another chance. Those are the bones, right?"

Gideon looked at this new member of his brotherhood. "Yeah, that's the gist."

"Okay, tell me more. What's she like? Why is she special?"

Gideon chewed his lower lip. He hated the attention of the AA meetings, hated opening himself up to people. Hated feeling silent judgement or — worse — pity. But the men before him were essentially his brothers and hadn't given him any of that bullshit. Being open with strangers was different than being open with family. Amy wanted him to work on not assuming everyone was going to hold his past against him. To trust that part of healing himself meant breaking down his walls. Max was a perfect test.

"My dad died when I was kid. I leaned on drugs and alcohol and eventually music. I'd... become closed off. I met Ella last year at a party, and she showed me light still existed in the world. But she didn't want to be around my, uh, habits, so we ended things before tour. I've been three months sober and we're talking again." He felt himself blush at the thought of being between her thighs, another form of talking.

Max nodded, understanding showing in his eyes. "I also lead the sober life and I respect you. Thank you for sharing." He turned to the other guys. "Okay, so I think we should add a low synth on top of the drums, and then maybe, like, an, 'Eh' vocal sound on every half note?"

Anthony adjusted his keyboard accordingly with the help of Max, and they played it over the drums.

"And then I'm thinking we change the sax to sound like this for the verse..." The notes were quick but blended nicely with the changed synth. "And then like this for the chorus..." He demonstrated longer, more sultry jazz notes. Gideon felt justice being done, and the smiles throughout the room reflected everyone else's excitement.

"Alright, let's record," he said, nodding to Tom behind the glass.

It felt good having magic back in his life, especially when it meant having Ella.

Nothing had been the same since she'd left.

Nothing would be the same with her back.

24

The smell of pizza wafted through Ella's apartment while she set the boxes on her counter, the sound of Julie and Rachel's laughter moving closer to where she stood. While they'd waited for the pizza, they all dove into their first solid glass of wine for Girl's Night and started watching a comedy. This was the first Girl's Night they'd included Rachel in and they didn't want to worry about missing crucial details in the movie if they ended up gabbing.

While Ella and Julie lived in their oldest, comfiest pajamas on these nights, Rachel had shown up dressed to impress, with her hair done and makeup in full glam mode. She'd kicked off her heels upon entering, gliding over the hardwood floors so few creaks occurred, exclaiming how "homey" the various items made the space feel.

Rachel came from money and Ella usually felt shabby in comparison. She took comfort in the fact that Rachel was always honest and her compliments genuine. Rachel eventually changed into her pajamas — a pretty pink silk — and still looked straight out of a luxury catalog.

"Oh, yum! I love that you guys do this, thank you so much for inviting me." Rachel's face lit up while she dished a couple slices of the gooey goodness.

"Girl, it was past time," Julie said on her way back to the couch.

The boxed wine sat on the coffee table to ensure easy access for all. They refilled their glasses, loosely paying attention to the TV screen.

"So, El, tell me more about Gideon. I know you didn't just talk." The words were barely understandable through Julie's full mouth.

They'd been trying to get Ella to talk all night, and her obvious blushing only spurred them on, no matter how many deflections she threw at them. Earlier that week, Rachel had pointed out she liked to keep her professional and personal lives somewhat separate. Ella told herself she didn't know how delving into her romantic details would impact her professional life with Rachel, that she didn't want to talk things up too much without knowing for sure where they were headed. But the pit in her stomach was there because she didn't want to admit to sleeping with the guy who'd broken her trust and her heart. She didn't want to face their judgement.

"You always think we did more than just talk," she said, trying to throw her best friend off.

Rachel laughed. "Ella, I haven't known you all that long and even I can deduce you didn't just talk. Also, we're talking about the same guy, right? I mean…" She drank from her glass, making eyes at how attractive Gideon was.

Ella busied herself with the pizza, hoping they'd get too consumed with the movie and would drop it. But they only watched her, expectant, occasionally drinking from their glasses. She'd always wanted a group of friends but had always been too busy to build one. What she wanted was staring her right in the face, if she was brave enough to see it.

"Fine," she said, sighing. "We didn't just talk."

"I knew it!" They squealed in unison, classic sleepover style.

She was surprised at their reaction. She knew if the roles were reversed, she'd be playing "mom" with her friend. Ella was relieved and caught them up about the coffee with Gideon, how his own admissions had made her realize her own walls.

How he'd taken care of her like a true gentleman and then how he'd taken care of her quite the opposite of that. They listened with rapt attention, making the occasional comment. When she was done, Ella took several gulps from her glass and turned to the TV. She had no idea what was happening in the movie. But watching the movie was better than confronting their potential judgement. She felt open.

Vulnerable.

An emotion she'd pushed down since she was a teenager, one she tried to swallow with another sip of wine.

"Well, that night sounds a lot more fun than my week," Rachel said. She stood and went to grab more pizza.

"Seriously. Just... be careful, El. He's messy," Julie sighed. "Speaking of messy, how's your mom?"

Julie knew Ella's mom, Margaret, was in and out of rehab. She knew Margaret was supposed to come home soon, but Ella hadn't told her about the last visit. The fear and loneliness she'd seen in her mom's face. The same fear and loneliness she'd seen in Gideon's face when she broke up with him.

"She's good," Ella said, knowing she'd have to call her mom to check in sooner rather than later.

Rachel waltzed back into the room, settling on the fluffy rug with two more slices. Ella used her entrance as an excuse to turn their attention to the movie and Rachel's lack of a dating life.

Some things she wasn't ready to be open about, and her mom was one of them.

25

Mornings were so much more enjoyable sober.

Gideon had traded waking up hungover at noon for meditation at 7 a.m. He traded morning scrolls through Instagram for reading an actual book. The late sunrise filtered through his living room windows, grazing the tops of the trees with an orange glow. He sipped his first mug of coffee and thought about his conversation with his mom the night before. Appreciated the strong liquid and her comforting words.

Appreciation was a big thing he'd had reinforced the last few months, something his mom had tried to share with him after the death of his father. But his rebellious and hurt teenage mind had blown it off and led him down a much darker path. Now, able to think straight and be open to healing, her words aligned with his recovery. Their weekly phone calls always helped him recenter. Paired with the AA meetings and his sponsor Amy, he felt stronger than ever. He'd gone to a meeting last night, having missed one last week, and was able to catch up with Amy. He felt less tense in the group than before and actually found himself enjoying some of the others he'd seen but rarely spoke to. A sense of rightness had settled over him over the past few days. He sent a silent thank you out into the ether, moving to the couch to read one of the books on his father's old coffee table.

Gideon wasn't sure how much time passed before his doorbell rang. He went to the apartment intercom, turning on the video to see who was interrupting his morning.

Ryan?

"Hey man, what's up?" Gideon couldn't hide the confusion from his voice. While he and Ryan were close, his bandmate had never shown up at his apartment except for parties or as a pickup to band practice.

"Hey! I just wanted to talk to you, do you have a minute?" Ryan shuffled on the other end of the feed.

"Sure, I'll buzz you up."

Gideon unlocked his apartment door and

poured some coffee for Ryan. The oven read 10 a.m., which was early by musician standards.

The footsteps on the stairs ended where the creak of his door began, and Gideon passed the steaming mug to his blond bandmate as he shut the door behind him.

"What's good, man? I wasn't sure you'd be up, it's early for you." Ryan smiled.

His comment hit Gideon with the realization that no one really knew him now that he was sober. Everyone probably only ever remembered him at 4 a.m., sloppy, or at 1 p.m., hurting and trying to make it through band practice.

"Ha, I've been waking up before 9 a.m. for months. Perk of being sober." Gideon sipped from his own mug on the way back to the couch. "This is a surprise, what can I do for you?"

Ryan cleared his throat, sitting on the opposite end of the couch. "So I was passing by your place on my way into Sugar Grove and wanted to check on you." He sipped from his mug, eyeing Gideon over the rim.

"Um, cool. I mean, I'm good. I'm great, Ryan. Why, what's up?"

"At the recording studio, what you said to Max? I dunno, it just kind of hit me. We're not as close as I thought. And, well, you know I try to stay sober more often than not." He looked away. "I guess what I'm trying to say is thank you for sharing and I know how hard it can be and, well, if you ever need a friend..."

Gideon looked at his friend, remembering when he'd met the man before him as a scrawny older teen. How they'd bonded — over emo music and missing parents and pot — while trying to fit in at college. Anthony had brought Ryan into their friend- ship, and Ryan had brought in Lucas. The four figured themselves out together, but Anthony had kept Gideon on the wild side while Lucas had kept Ryan on the more straight and narrow.

"Thanks, man. I really appreciate that." Gideon sipped his coffee, gathering the courage to keep the conversation going. He liked the idea of being even closer with his bandmates. He liked the idea of not being so isolated.

"To be honest... it's been lonely. I guess I always thought we were close because of college but it's really been years since we've hung out one-on-one. And yeah, being sober does change things. It changes me."

"I get that. It's hard for me to drink after being

sober for a time. Would you be interested in asking Tom to make it a dry tour?"

Gideon's head snapped to face his friend. "What tour?"

"What do you mean? Didn't Tom call you?" Ryan set his mug down on the coffee table before pulling out his phone and playing a voicemail out loud.

Gideon pulled out his phone, realizing he hadn't checked it since the night before in an effort to enjoy his morning. Tom had also left him a voicemail with the same information.

Band practice tomorrow.

Headlining festival tour that upcoming summer.

26

Her phone stared at her from the coffee table, and Ella could only stare back. After Rachel and Julie left that morning, she'd gone over the inevitable phone call with her mom in her head, how her mom would sound and what she'd say. She watched Pollack strut over and sit at her feet. He stared at her.

Ella rolled her eyes. "Yeah, yeah. I'm getting there."

Taking a deep breath, she found the rehab's contact info. Her thumb hovered over the call button while she tried to steel herself. A soft rub against her leg eased her anxiety, and she pulled the trigger. She gave her mom's name to the receptionist and waited to jazz music for her mom's voice to come through.

"Ella?"

Gravelly and warm. Healthy.

"Hey, mom."

Ella's voice felt small to her own ears, and she curled deeper under the blanket without disturbing Pollack, who was sprawled on top of her feet.

"Hi, sweetie." Margaret's voice was at once foreign and comforting. Ella never knew how to feel about these weekly phone calls, knowing how far away her mom was.

But also how safe.

Ella took a deep breath, ignoring the question weighing on her mind. "How are things? Did you talk to someone about the lack of quality in the food, as you so kindly put it?"

"Oh, *did* I!" The timidity from her mom's voice dissipated. "I swear, the minute someone raises a fuss no one does anything. But give a celebrity name and they'll give it on a silver platter." She laughed her movie star laugh. The forced one.

"Of course you'd get it upgraded." Ella laughed along, leaning into the arm of her sofa.

"Ah, you know me. If it's not a hotel, is it even worth it?" Margaret let the question hang between them. "So, kid, tell me what's new. You know how they are about cellphones and shit."

The only stability Ella had felt growing up was her friendship with her mother. The guys her mom paraded around, the ones that stuck for a short time, the ones who were mean, they would all come and go. But when Margaret needed a friend, Ella was there. And when Ella needed a friend, Margaret ditched her poor attempts at being a mother and became the friend Ella needed. As she grew up and started taking responsibility for her mother's actions, Ella had to take on the role of parent. But old habits die hard and confiding in her mom as a friend was one of them.

"Well, business is really good. Like, really really good." Ella took a deep breath. "Rachel and I are actually looking into moving to New York City in the next few months." Ella exhaled slowly, glad to get it off her chest. While she rarely saw her mom who lived a couple towns over, she felt bad at choosing to be even farther away. She wouldn't be able to drive by to check in on Margaret. It'd be more difficult to visit her on her next rehab trip. And there was something else, an ache settling in her heart, at being away from her mom. Ella felt herself choke up at the thought.

"See, I always knew you were destined to get out of that podunk town. You're too good for that place. Time for you to really show the world what you've got."

"Yeah, I'm working on it, mom." The choke Ella had felt rising released.

"I know you are but it's my job to make sure you're an active member of society. I mean, when I was your age I was already married, planning on you, and had an Oscar nomination under my belt. I just want to make sure you won't regret anything by taking your sweet time growing up."

Ella closed her eyes, trying to ignore the heat washing over her. Her not moving fast enough was a constant point of contention, one her mom was more than happy to bring up any chance she could.

"I'm not going to argue with you right now. The point is I've *been* an active member of society, just not in the way you approve of." Ella took a deep breath, trying to center herself. "I'll never be a famous actress, but I will be myself. Could you please let it go and just be happy for me?"

Her mom sighed on the other end. "Fine. I guess when you make this big move you won't be able to visit me here, will you?"

Ella rolled her eyes, shifting Pollack off her feet so she could burn the adrenaline building from her mom's comments.

"Mom, you don't like it when I visit you now. And

besides, you'll be out soon and then you can come visit me instead."

Only Margaret's breathing was audible on the other end. Ella paced the living room waiting for her response.

"You are coming home soon, right?"

"I'm just not sure when, Ella. Okay?" Her mom's voice was hollow, far away. "Come visit me next month and we'll talk about it."

Ella stopped in her tracks, staring at the worn wood floors, her mother's words heard but not registered. As so often happened when faced with her mom, the fight left Ella and exhaustion hit instead. She learned to pick her battles, no matter how few and far between they were.

"Okay. I'll talk to you next week."

27

Gideon looked around his apartment for the hundredth time, hoping it was good enough for Ella. Ryan's visit yesterday had thrown him off, but since it would be Ella's first time in his apartment, he lost himself in scrubbing the kitchen down three times and mopping the floors twice as much.

What his home lacked in character was made up for by the shiny features. Features the rent was really going to each month. Large windows throughout, the ones in the living room overlooking a small forest behind the building. Being on the fourth floor allowed for ample sunlight and limited traffic noise, perfect for the open floor plan. The newly renovated kitchen with stainless steel appliances and an island didn't hurt either. When he'd signed the lease, he dreamed of using the kitchen to learn how to cook.

Meeting Ella last year had spurred that dream into action, and he'd only gotten better. Gideon fingered the heirloom coffee table and glanced at his dad's old electric bass behind the sectional, hanging in the center of the wall above his makeshift instrument storage. It was the only piece of art he needed in his home. He adjusted the throw pillows he'd gotten that week for the occasion, checked the time, and did one last pass through the bedroom and bathroom.

Immaculate.

He bounced over the antique patterned rug in the living room, waiting for her to arrive while trying to push down the ache of missing whiskey. He'd gotten rid of his bar cart the night before tour, not wanting to be tempted when he got back. Wanting to be the man he promised himself he could be. But he had yet to replace it with something less tempting, and the empty space against the wall only served to taunt him.

The buzz of the building intercom jolted him from his anxiety. He ran to buzz Ella up, waiting as the sound of her steps grew steadily louder. She rapped on the door at the same time as he opened it, catching her by surprise. Her eyes went wide before she started laughing at the coincidence and leaned in to give him a hug.

"Good timing, eh? It's nice to see you," he murmured into the top of her head as he held her soft body against him.

"Hmmm, always." Her words were barely audible, lips pressed against his chest. Ella released her arms and looked at him, her delicate face upturned. Gideon lowered his lips to hers, grazing their fullness, inhaling her warm scent. He settled his forehead against hers and looked into her bright eyes.

"Are you gonna let me in, handsome?" she asked.

"I guess we'd be more comfortable that way, huh?" He gave her lips one last longing kiss, feeling her sink into him.

He was never going to let her go.

"Seriously, Gideon." She pulled herself away, a soft smile on her lips.

He thread his fingers through hers, pulling her through the threshold into the quiet part of his world. Their hands stayed entwined as her head turned to survey the space, taking in the sectional, the musical instruments behind it lined up in stands against the dark gray wall. A tall bookshelf held a sampling of books, the TV stand empty of DVDs. Ella moved into the kitchen, her hand relaxing against his but not letting go. She walked around the island, stopping at his old friend, the taunting empty space.

"What goes here?" She turned to look at him, her voice betraying what she already knew.

"Well, that was my bar area but... Ya know." He felt heat rising in his cheeks and his hand tensed around hers. She leaned her head against his shoulder.

"Maybe a coffee area? A big plant? Maybe something fresh to bring some life to the canvas." She kissed his shoulder, releasing his hand before moving down the hall, trailing her hand along the wall.

Gideon leaned against the island, watching her. Taking in the woman before him, her strength set in the way she carried herself, hair catching the light in a halo he always loved. She moved slowly, confidently, lush hips swaying with every step toward the bedroom. Pausing in the door frame, she flashed a smile at Gideon before disappearing into the room.

He had no choice but to follow.

28

She'd been surprised by the dark, sterile energy of his apartment. Dark walls, empty shelves, spotless counters. Trying to find elements of the man she knew in the common spaces, elements of the man that had dad jokes aplenty and was inked in spiritual symbols, but those components had been relegated to the bedroom.

Ella had to pause at the doorframe to take in the room before her, especially when greeted with the centerpiece: a king-sized bed. She'd flashed him a smile, hoping it came off as suggestively as she felt, before moving past it to explore the other objects in the room.

Stacks and stacks of books littered the floor beneath the two large windows. She knelt before them, craned her neck to read the titles, traced her fingers along the various spines. A creak let Ella know Gideon had made his way to the door, but she was still enamored with the sheer volume of books before her. Old, new, hardcover, softcover, what looked like two different tablets. She stood and moved to the dresser across from the foot of the monstrous bed.

A yoga mat leaned against the simple black dresser. Trinkets were arranged carefully on the dresser's surface, reminiscent of the ones she had in front of her full-length mirror back at her apartment. She picked up the familiar statue of Ganesha, the remover of obstacles, Gideon's a black stone while hers was ivory in color. Ella set it down and fingered the surrounding crystals and other statues.

Creaks gave way to his spicy musk inundating her senses. Gideon's tattooed arms snaked their way around her waist, his face nuzzling her neck. He took a deep breath and released it with a kiss on her neck. A move that always caused her nipples to harden and a heat to flush between her thighs. She sighed, leaned against him, wrapped her arms around his.

"I missed you." The words snuck out before she

could stop them. Until they could settle where they stood with each other, she didn't want to show all her cards. But there was something about him that always managed to break down her defenses, to pull out the most honest of disclosures.

Gideon inhaled deeper. "You have no idea, darlin'."

His pet name for her reached right into her heart and pulled. She'd missed the way it rolled off his tongue, like he'd sculpted each letter as a gift for her. Needing to fall a little more, she turned in his arms. His eyes granted her wish as she saw the love they held. Ella wanted to pretend her move to New York City wasn't happening, that they could hold onto what they had in that moment. But falling into him also meant opening for him to fall also, and she couldn't do that without sorting out where they stood.

"Wanna snuggle on the bed and catch up on some things? I feel like I haven't seen you in forever," she whispered, looping her arms around his neck.

"Obviously having you in my bed is the only thing I want to do." Gideon swung them around, never letting her go as he picked her up and waddled to the bed, falling into the pillowy comforter. They laughed at the force and readjusted until they were properly wrapped around one another. Ella kissed his broad chest, imagining the smooth muscles beneath his thin T-shirt. She kissed the dip between his pecs, one hand running its way down his back.

"El, we're going back on tour in the summer."

The words caught her breath but her hand kept moving, not wanting to betray her surprise. She knew it had to happen sometime, and of course summer would be festival season. They could headline with their new album and drum up fans before they released their second one. But hearing one of her biggest fears blurted out loud was another monster, and she still had to introduce hers.

"I... I figured as much. Part of being a rockstar, right? Festival season?" She squeezed him tighter against her.

"Yeah, a little bit," he said, sighing, pulling back and placing his hand on her cheek. "We can make this work, right? I mean, I know it's months away. But still."

The space between his forehead was creased, and when she placed her hand on his neck, she felt his pulse racing. Ella bit her lower lip, knowing she'd only add to the furrow.

"Rachel and I are moving to New York City. I'm not really sure when, but it's looking like in the next four to six months. We're just waiting on a big client to sign."

The crease disappeared as surprise crossed his features.

"Ella, that's amazing! When will you know about the client?"

Breaking their gaze, she looked toward his ceiling, trying to recall their meeting with Charlie.

"Monday. Tomorrow," she said to the space above her, unable to bear coming to a conclusion about her and the only man she'd ever loved.

"Wow, I'm so happy for you." Gideon propped himself up on his elbow. "Business must be good, it'll be so nice to get out of this small town. You deserve so much more."

"Thanks... But what does that mean for us?"

He shifted so he was positioned over her, lips a hair's width from hers.

"Ella, I want you. I've always wanted you. New York City's not only very close, but I'm from there. It would make sense for a rising band to live in a place that offers anonymity. We've discussed it abstractly. I'm sure before or after the summer, the guys would want to move."

The invisible pressure from her chest started to lift as she thought through the logistics. It all made sense. And it was all doable.

She smiled, pressing herself against him, inviting his lips to close the gap.

29

Her lips beckoned Gideon and he had no choice but to oblige.

His tongue breached their softness to explore the warmth inside. Ella's fingers tangled in his hair and pulled him closer while his hands roamed her perfect curves. It wasn't long before they were both panting, frantically trying to strip the other of their clothes. Gideon sat up and climbed off the bed, pulling her with him. He lifted her dress over her head, kissing her exposed chest tenderly. Enjoying every inch of heated skin. He kissed the length of her body, kneeling before her. He held her lush thighs in his hands, kissing the area around her fragrant core, teasing the lacy waistband of her panties with his fingertips. She moaned his name and threaded her fingers harder through his hair.

"Baby, I need to worship you." He gazed up at her, stroking the side of her legs, enjoying the tremble in her legs when he grazed the back of her knees. She looked down at him with hooded eyes.

"I'll never say no to you."

Their eyes were locked as he peeled away her wet panties, paradise so close he could taste it.

And taste Gideon did, leaning her back onto the bed while he spread her legs. Her scent called to him, a rising primal need that could only be quenched with her nectar. He put his face against her heat, breathing deeply, licking her slick folds slowly, enjoying how she tensed in his hands. He took his time, relishing her small moans, his name on her tongue, before his own need to devour her pushed through.

He toyed her swollen clit with the tip of his tongue and wasted no time with inserting three fingers. She gasped at the sudden intrusion, her hot pussy clenching around him with pleasure. Her hands twisted the sheets as she pushed her hips even closer to him. He pressed the pads of his fingers against her innermost sensitive spot, his eyes never leaving her face as she arched against him. He thrust his fingers in and out of her wet sheath while his tongue worked her tender bud.

Every pant of hers caused him to move faster, bringing her to the edge. When her legs started shaking, he knew he was close to bringing her the euphoria she deserved. Gideon pumped until he felt her molten release, her essence coating his hand. He coaxed her to the end, helping her ride the waves of pleasure until her muscles stopped clenching.

"Come here." Her voice came out as a rasp, her hands clutching his shoulders. Still between her legs, Gideon smiled, kissing her inner thighs. She stared at him through half-closed eyes, a lazy smile playing on her lips.

"Not yet, darlin'. I think we need to get you clean," he said. Gideon bent over her, kissing and nipping at her soft stomach. His fingers found their way to her dripping core and teased her opening. He swiped his tongue one final time through her folds before rising, pulling her off the bed. Ella stood on her tiptoes to lace her arms around his neck, kissing him fully. He sank into her, holding her as close to him as he could. But he needed to slide his hands over her wet curves, to lick the rivulets off her chest. He needed to bend her over and see that sweet ass bounce against him while he fucked her.

He leaned forward, his hands falling to the

perfect crease where her ass met her thighs, pulling her legs apart.

She laughed mid-kiss. "Oh, do you want me to jump?"

"Maybe," he said, "If we're going to shower, I need to be at least a little dirty."

Ella jumped, her legs hugging his hips, nestling his cock between her heat and his belly. Being that close to her center, bare, made his cock throb. Her breasts pressing against his chest didn't help.

Neither did holding her ass.

Or the thoughts of what he wanted to do to her.

30

Straddling Gideon while he carried her so easily to the bathroom was something that should've been on Ella's bucket list.

She didn't know why up until now it hadn't been, or why it'd taken them so long to explore the shower together.

Holding his chiseled body between her legs brought a fresh wave of lust to shoot through her aching frame. She'd forgotten the strength of the orgasms he gave her, how they rolled through her body like a summer thunderstorm and lingered just as long. She'd forgotten how being close to him made her want a never-ending rain.

He set her gently on the counter, and she jumped with the sudden cold against her flushed skin. But when he turned around to turn on the water, the shock dissipated, replaced with an inferno. His muscular backside rippled, his ass round and begging to be grabbed. Ella slid off the ledge and stroked the length of his spine with her fingertip. Gideon turned to face her. His hand, dripping, tangled in her hair as he gazed into her eyes. Never looking away, Ella crouched to her knees. From the floor, he was reminiscent of a Greek god. Tall, all muscle and man.

Facing his enormous cock helped with the impression.

She grabbed his shaft, her small hand covering only a portion of all he offered, and took his tip between her lips. Her tongue swirled, catching the drop of essence formed at the peak. Gideon hissed, his hand gripping her hair even tighter. No matter how big the man, Ella always felt powerful in this position. She relished the way she could bring a man to his knees while being on hers, how the way she touched and licked him brought him ultimate pleasure.

She inched him farther into her mouth, her tongue moving against him, drawing him in. When her lips barely met his base, she pushed herself to take him even deeper before pulling him out quickly. The shock from the cold air after being in her warm, wet mouth caused Gideon to gasp. Moving her hand up and down his wet length, she took him in her mouth again, releasing and taking his cock until his knees shook. Her other hand cupped his balls, heavy, pulling and massaging while she worked his length.

"Ella..." he moaned. "I'm close, don't stop."

The magic words hit Ella's ears and she slowed down, removing him from her grip as she looked up. His face was twisted in confusion. She kissed her way up his body, meeting his lips with hers.

"I'm on the pill," she whispered between kisses. "And —- if you're clean — I need you to fuck me. In the shower."

He responded with an urgent kiss, his hands pulling her hair, pulling her head closer against his. Her hands roamed his body, stroking the tapered waist, the back and shoulders she'd dreamt of. His shaft pressed against her belly, pushing into her with a hardness she needed elsewhere. They climbed into the shower, the steam from the hot water swirling around them.

Ella took a step back from him. The water flattened his hair, the longer pieces on top falling in his eyes, water dripping down his cheeks. His eyes bore into hers, sapphires filled with lust. The shower beat against his shoulders, the water sluicing down his pecks, his washboard abs creating natural rivers leading to his cock protruding from his body. An invitation. A beacon.

She smiled and stepped into his inked arms.

This man was hers.

31

Gideon knew there was no goddess in existence like the one before him.

The water from the shower barely touched her golden curves, but as she stood watching him, the spray was enough to form delicate pearls across her skin. Gems he wanted to lick off and collect, hold the taste of her for the rest of his life.

He held out his arm and she stepped forward with a knowing smile. Leaning down to kiss her, his member pressed against her belly as she snaked her arms around his neck. The water met their skin with heated force, only adding to their eternal inferno, mixing with their frantic gropes and sloppy kisses. Gideon spun the woman he loved around, pressing her against the opposite wall. Her curves were even more beautiful from behind, a slender waist ending in wide hips. Ella arched her back, glancing at him over her shoulder.

"Just make sure you spank me," she said.

His cock throbbed at her words.

"Darlin', I want to do more than just spank you."

He twisted her wet hair around his fist, arching her back even more. His hand grabbed her ass before trailing to her pussy spread before him. Gideon grabbed his cock, stroking the hard length before pressing the tip to her opening. Ella wiggled her hips back, taking a little more of him inside her. He pulled her hair, thrusting his cock inside her with one swift motion, causing her to gasp. He groaned as her wet heat enveloped him and looked down at where his hips met her full cheeks.

Gideon watched his cock slowly moving out of her, glistening with her juices. He gripped her ass in his hand, thrusting into her, causing her to whimper. He found a rhythm, his hand occasionally tugging her hair. His other hand rubbed her ass, waiting for the right moment to fulfill her wish.

The water splashed against their moving bodies, jumping and adding to the slapping of Gideon's pelvis against her. Ella's panting grew more heated, her moans more frequent. Gideon spanked one round cheek, causing her to jump.

And beg for more.

He slapped her ass again, speeding up his pumping. "You like that, baby?" he groaned. "You like feeling how hard you get me?"

She moaned, moving her hips in time with his. "You know I love feeling your hard cock in my tight pussy, Gideon."

"I want to make you cum all over me," he said. He released her hair, moving faster and harder against her. She was a dream come true, and he wanted her to feel pleasure shoot through her body. And her heart.

He folded over her, his fingers finding her clit. The contact made her cry out, her tightening muscles bringing him closer to the edge.

"Cum with me, baby," he murmured into her shoulder.

The words broke the dam. He felt her surge around him and his own release followed. They pulsed together, heaving beneath the hot water beating down on them. They stilled against the tiled wall, joined as one. Gideon wrapped his arms around Ella's waist and leaned his cheek against her back. He slipped out of her when she turned around but her smile offered a different kind of warmth.

"I could get used to this, Ella."

Her green eyes were bright against his darker, wet hair. They softened with his admission and she leaned into him. They held each other beneath the pounding water, and Gideon knew there was no other woman he could ever be with.

All he needed was a ring.

32

Ella gazed at him from across the island. They were perched on bar stools while eating takeout Indian food for dinner, of which Gideon was happy to shovel with few breaths in between. He was fully absorbed in mixing the tikka masala sauce with rice and she was trying to be fully absorbed in getting used to this. Them, together. Since he'd gotten back, being with him had been easy. She was able to bare herself, body and soul, and he was able to do the same in return. She'd never laughed as much as she did when she was with him.

And she'd never felt safer.

But Ella just couldn't ignore the small voice in the back of her mind, the one telling her she couldn't be safe with anyone. That eventually, they all turn around and hurt you.

She took a bite of her aloo gobi, chewing slowly while trying not to think of her mom and all the relationships she'd been through. Of all the different men that had made Ella feel special and then disappeared. How Gideon had already disappeared once.

"Whatchya thinking about, darlin'?"

Gideon's voice tore through Ella's thoughts and she blinked to clear his image before her.

"Nothing." She picked at her food. "What about you?"

He set down his fork. "That doesn't sound like nothing."

"No, really. I'm just tired," she said. She took another bit of her food, throwing him a smile. "You really worked me."

"Just doing my job." Gideon winked. "I'm always here if you need to talk." He dug back into his plate.

Ella chuckled, picking at her food some more. Her thoughts and feelings were things she had to figure out on her own. She didn't want to turn this into a big thing with Gideon when it was her own wall to tear down. She'd never seen a real, loving relationship before, let alone been in one. How did you let go enough to trust someone with your heart? How did you let go enough to trust someone who's broken it once before, but seems to have changed?

Gideon sighed, stretching. His plate was practically licked and Ella set her fork down in response.

"Thanks for a lovely dinner." He set his chin in his hand, batting his eyelashes at her. "I felt so wined and dined."

Ella laughed, rising to clear the dishes. Gideon was rarely a goof but it was one of her favorite sides of his.

"Well, you're the one who bought so I think I'm the one who's supposed to feel wined and dined. Thanks for the great food and even better company." She planted a kiss on his shoulder on her way to the sink. Exhaustion seeped into her body while she washed the plates and silverware, muscles pleasantly aching from the way Gideon had pounded into her. Her ass was a little tender from his spanks, but the post-shower kisses he'd dropped on the red mark had helped replace the sting with a slow burn.

Gideon came up on her side, drying the dishes with a towel. Ella looked up at him and smiled. His hair was mostly dried and fairly rumpled, his body hidden by a loose tee and baggy sweatpants, his face relaxed and focused on the task at hand. She loved seeing his tenderness, how she could see him how he'd been at eight and how he'd be in five years.

Ella dried her hands before touching his bicep,

rippling beneath his skin with the motions of drying the last dish. She traced the vine surrounding the monkey deity Hanuman while he folded the damp towel and hung it back on the stove handle. She never tired of following the lines in his body and seeing where they ended. She kissed the portrait, Gideon placing a kiss on her head in return.

"C'mon, beautiful. Let's snuggle."

He grabbed her hand and led her to the bed she'd been dreaming about since she arrived.

33

Gideon slowly opened his eyes, taking in the muted daylight streaming around his blackout shades.

He had his woman curled up against him after they'd spent hours exploring one another, riding wave after wave of pleasure before sinking into exhausted bliss. They had talked until the twilight hours of the morning, opening their hearts and allowing each other in. She had told him she wanted, needed, to move to New York City. Gideon had known at some point Eternal Youths would have to move to a bigger city, but until she'd brought it up, those plans had been off in the distance. Now he felt like he had more of a purpose, a goal to reach if they were going to make this work for real.

Ella shifted, burrowing deeper into his chest, a faint sigh escaping. He tightened his arms around her and dropped a soft kiss on her forehead. She'd gone into her childhood, her struggles with her mom and learning how to be her own woman. When Gideon had pressed her about her current relationship with Margaret, she'd brushed it off and turned to his relationship with his mom. He peered down at her sleeping form, making a mental note to ask her again.

For the first time, Gideon felt a new wave of emotion overcoming him. He closed his eyes, breathing in the scent of sandalwood and vanilla.

Safety.

The elusive security he'd been trying to obtain was finally here. No amount of drugs or alcohol had brought it. No number of yoga classes or guided meditations had delivered it, even if they'd opened the door. He drifted through the warmth enveloping him, realizing the peace he sought was here because he was here. After opening himself fully to Ella, he had reached the place of releasing his father, of forgiving his mother, of loving himself. Of enjoying the moment he was in.

It didn't hurt having the love of his life nestled in his bed.

Gideon had tried to hide his concern at her plan to move to New York City. He needed to figure out how moving would fit into asking her to marry him.

He gently reached over Ella to check the time on his phone. Tom had called a band practice for noon and would probably give more details regarding their summer tour. It was still early morning, he had some time. Gideon looked around the bed, trying to determine how to remove his big frame from Ella's without waking her. He wanted coffee and breakfast to be ready for when she woke.

Swinging one leg out of the covers, he inched himself away from the glow of her body, missing it the second they were separated. He moved slowly, rearranging the covers and pillows to provide some semblance of him beside her. He slid off the bed, donning pajamas and a sweater, partially closing the door on his way to the kitchen.

The air was cold in comparison to the haven he'd come from. Gideon shivered while digging through his fridge, pulling out the components to a good breakfast. It wouldn't be his mom's French toast, but it would still be a cozy meal.

He brewed coffee, chopping the potatoes to roast with garlic and rosemary. Bacon was next. One of the things he loved about cooking was being able to eat along the way, and the butter was no exception. It'd

always been a favorite of his, and he popped a table-
spoon in his mouth while he flipped the sizzling
strips.

"Was that... butter?"

Gideon turned. Ella stood behind him, clutching
one of his sweaters around her. Glassy eyes, tousled
hair, gravelly voice. His kryptonite.

"Good morning to you, too," he said, smiling and
turning back to the popping bacon.

She noiselessly came up behind him. Her small
hands ran their way up his back, pressing into his
shoulders and lats for a mini massage. He felt a
smaller press between his shoulder blades. A kiss.
Her arms wrapped around his waist.

"Good morning," she mumbled. "You didn't
answer me. Did I just see you, Gideon Pike, eat a slab
of butter?"

He couldn't stop a laugh from escaping as he
pulled the bacon from the pan. "It's certainly possible. Want a slice?" The bacon was hot between his
fingers as he offered her one of the crispy bits. She
released him, taking the greasy goodness and
moving to his elbow.

"Can I help? I feel like you're always making me
food." She glanced up at him, her mouth full.

"Absolutely not. I love making you food. And I

enjoy your company." He kissed her forehead, dropping the spinach and some spices into the bacon grease sitting in the pan.

"Okay, but I want — nay, need — to know more about this butter habit of yours."

34

How someone could eat butter straight up confused the shit out of Ella.

The fact it was the love of her life was another matter.

She sat at the island, watching Gideon's perfectly sculpted back while he worked. Rosemary and bacon odors drifted through the air and her stomach grumbled. The coffee he'd made was perfect, with just a hint of cinnamon. Ella nursed her mug.

She was home.

The previous night had tumbled into her morning, the words they spoke and the ones they didn't need to. They were both a bit gun-shy emotionally but understanding of the other's hesitance to deep dive, which only made them want to trust the other more. It was clear they were in it, together, until the end. Whenever that was or however it came about. That they could find a way through any issue. That he was the only man she'd ever truly love.

"Breakfast is served, darlin'." Gideon turned with two plates in hand, setting one before her. Roasted potatoes, sautéed spinach, perfectly cooked eggs over medium, crispy bacon for her and fatty bacon for him. She tore her gaze from the food to his face.

"I know you cook for me but it really never ceases to amaze me. This looks delicious, thank you."

His lips quirked. "Anything, anytime, for you." He sat across from her and dug into the bacon. She watched the grease wet his lips, his tongue slipping to lick them. Wanting to be the one to lick them clean while she straddled him.

"Take a picture, it'll last longer." He winked.

Ella felt her entire body flush, from being caught ogling him and from the steamy thoughts coursing through her mind.

"Sorry, I was just thinking about how I could get you back into bed." She raised her eyebrows and took a bite.

"Maybe a quickie but I have band practice. And I'm pretty sure you have a big call today, right? I wouldn't want to distract you," he said. "Again."

Oh, shit.

She'd forgotten about the phone call with Rachel and Charlie. She glanced at the time on the oven and started to hurry through her food. She needed to bring her A-game to the meeting, to show Rachel she was serious. To prove to herself she could do this.

"Ah, yes. Couldn't have your sexy ass distracting me from work, now can we?"

"No more than necessary, I'm afraid. But maybe we could plan a longer time this weekend?" He scooped the rest of his food onto his fork, taking the huge bite without losing any morsels, pleading eyes meeting hers.

Ella mentally went through her schedule. "I think I could do Saturday and/or Sunday, if that works for you?" Rachel had mentioned needing to look at office spaces in New York City but that was dependent on the call today.

"Perfect, I can't wait to do all sorts of things to you." His grin turned suggestive and he came to her side. As if reading her mind, he leaned in to give her a kiss, deep and full. He broke away and rested his forehead against hers.

"I love you. Always have, always will."

His eyes bore into hers and begged for another

kiss, another night, another year. She kissed him back and her hands found their way to his neck, pulling him closer into her.

Breathless, she let him go. "I love you. Always have, always will."

His hand grazed her cheek before he turned to clear their empty plates. Setting them in the sink, he walked back to the island and stretched, giving Ella a glimpse of his V. She reached out and pulled him between her legs. Ran her hands along his chiseled torso.

Sometimes she really couldn't believe this hot, sexy, kind man existed.

And she really couldn't believe that he was hers.

35

Having Max the saxophonist in the practice space was a welcome change no one had anticipated, least of all Gideon. The record label had liked the direction Eternal Youths was taking with their first full-length album, so Tom suggested incorporating Max's sax into a couple of the other songs to help make the sound consistent. Then, for the second album, Max would formally be a part of the band.

Max's deep laugh rang out at something Ryan had said, Lucas following suit. Gideon sipped his seltzer, watching them goof off. Tom had pulled Anthony into the hallway, his abandoned beer sitting on the table with copies of their lyrics. A reminder of an old life. Gideon picked it up and, realizing it was empty, tossed it.

He didn't need a reminder.

Tom and Anthony came back into the room, Tom running his hand through his hair. Anthony's face was red, eyes glazed as he stormed to his guitar. He plucked the strings wildly with his back turned to the group. The guys passed glances to one another before turning to Tom for instructions. The older man stood with his hands on his hips, graying hair catching the light. He looked tired.

"Alright, guys. We have all twelve songs for the album done, we just need to pick a couple to incorporate sax. We have recording time booked for Friday so we can get this to the label."

"Can you tell us more about this tour?" Ryan asked over Anthony's increasingly loud strums.

"Sure," Tom said, sighing. "It's October now, 4AD wants to release the album in January. Kind of like a new year, new band kind of thing. They're already working on press junkets. Instead of a headlining tour, they booked you on the festival circuit. The summer tour will be early May through late August, hitting all the major music festivals in the U.S. to drum up your fan base. We're working on filling space between those so we can just be on the road straight during those three or four months. Does that sound good to everyone?" He quickly glanced around. "Okay, good. Now what are your thoughts on songs to rework?"

The guys stood, nodding while they processed the new information. A piece of cake in light of the last tour opening for The National in the United States and throughout Europe.

Max spoke up. "Might I make a suggestion?"

The guys looked at him, and even Anthony stopped playing. "I know we're rockstars and all, but what are everyone's thoughts on making it a dry tour?"

Gideon's skin crawled as the anxiety spread through him. Max had gone about this without taking into account everyone's relationship with one another. Gideon had planned on asking Tom privately so as to not put anyone on the spot. That someone being Anthony. His cousin had always been Gideon's party partner, but ever since Gideon went sober, Anthony had delved into his bad habits harder than before. Gideon hadn't wanted to admit it, but after Tom asked him to keep an eye on Anthony, it was unmistakable. Tom seemed at a loss as to what to do with his son.

"Um, well, Max," Tom began, growing an inch when he crossed his arms, "We can certainly discuss it at a later date."

"Yeah, man. That's cool. I just know me and Gideon are sober and Ryan and Lucas try to be."

Gideon caught Ryan and Lucas glance at each other before he looked at the ground, not wanting to be brought into this conversation.

"And who are you?" Anthony broke the silence but not the tension. He walked up to Max, almost toe to toe. They rivaled each other in stature, but Anthony had a palpable energy that engulfed everyone in the room.

"Hey, man," Max said as he put his hands up, taking a couple steps back. "I know I'm new here but I figured it'd throw it out there since four of us follow that lifestyle. I thought a dry tour would make things easier for everyone."

Gideon watched the two stand off, remembering his own attitude when he'd drink. How confrontational or pissy he'd get. Being on the outside looking in was another wake-up call he hadn't known he needed. Seeing Anthony like this reinforced his gratitude at being able to take the step of getting clean, no matter how hard it'd been. How hard it sometimes still was.

"Guys, c'mon. We can definitely talk about it, it's not a bad idea." Tom walked to them slowly, placing a hand on their shoulders. Gideon knew the weight of it, of Tom's presence, fatherly in every hard and comforting aspect, would help diffuse the situation. At least for now.

"Fine." Anthony brushed the hand from his shoulder, riffing on his guitar.

Max nodded, picking up his sax. "Sure thing, man. Sorry for stepping on toes."

"K, now that we've made up, can we please get to work?" Lucas said from behind his drums.

Gideon polished off his seltzer and picked up his guitar. They all needed to get their heads clear if they were going to do this. Practice, the album, tour. Meeting — or better yet, exceeding — 4AD's expectations.

And he still needed to talk to them about moving.

36

"Hi Charlie, how are you?" Rachel's voice was steady, cheerful. "It's Rachel and Ella from Maven Media."

Ella sat beside her friend, picking at her nails while the phone sat between them, on speaker. She'd gotten to the office in the late morning and they'd been able to prep for the call. Signing Blue Bird Books would give them the money they needed to move to New York City and establish themselves as a boutique publicity firm.

"Hey, Rachel! Nice to hear from you." Charlie's voice crackled through the phone. "How is everyone?"

Ella shook her head at Charlie's omission of her name.

"We're good! We're excited to discuss moving forward with you," Rachel said. She leaned forward, her chair squeaking with the shift, her heels stuck in the carpet. Ella had kicked off her heels as soon as she'd walked into the office. Bare feet were optimal for swiveling in desk chairs to minimize anxiety.

"Likewise! We liked your proposal, Rachel. The price is a little more steep than we expected but I believe it's worth it. I spoke with our legal team about the contract and they wanted to review some things with your legal team before signing."

They heard shuffling paper on the other end of the call. Ella glanced at her friend before responding, wanting to participate so Rachel felt she was in on the partnership.

"Hi Charlie, it's Ella. That's not an issue at all, did you have any dates in mind?"

More shuffling. "Hi Ella. We'd like to review the contract as early as possible and ideally we'd sign in the next couple weeks, by the end of October. I'm assuming we'll all be 100% in on this?"

Ella ignored the icier tone Charlie had adopted. "Absolutely. How does Monday of next week look for you?" Rachel pulled out her planner, sharing the pages with her before Ella continued. "We'd also like to have this wrapped and ready as soon as possible."

"Good. I don't work with those who can't keep up. I was thinking we'll send you changes to the contract, your team will review, and we can discuss via phone. Would Friday work?"

Ella bristled at her comment. Out of her periphery, she saw Rachel glance at her but ignored it. They commiserated on times, Rachel texting Julie for her availability, and settled on that Friday at 2 p.m.

"Great. Thank you, ladies. I know we have to go over the finer details but I am excited to work with you. Have a great week!"

"Likewise, Charlie. Thank you!" Rachel ended the call.

Ella stared at the phone screen. Calming herself from Charlie's comments, processing what this meant.

Rachel leaned back in her chair and swiveled to face Ella, who didn't return the swivel. "I'm sorry about her attitude. That was rude."

"It's okay, I understand where she's coming from. She's trying to run a business. Just like we are." Ella chewed her lower lip, the reality of the conversation finally hitting her. The anxiety over the dreaded phone call, after she'd almost lost the account, was morphing into an anxiety filled with excitement. With purpose. She swiveled to face her business partner, her friend. Ella took in her pristine appearance, her strong posture, knowing there was no one else she'd rather work beside. She smiled.

"I guess we're moving to New York City."

Rachel beamed. "I guess we're moving to New York City."

37

Gideon had never been to The Lava Java. Even though Ella had worked there last year before he'd left on tour, she always worked the morning or afternoon shifts. The shifts during which he was either sleeping, hungover, or at band practice.

He walked through the heavy oak doors, greeted with the smell of coffee and the soft chatter of friends hanging out. The spacious building had been around since the 1950's and had once served as a pharmacy. Over its lifetime, it had been renovated several times. Its latest incarnation — a hipster coffee shop — was complete with a copper tin ceiling and thrifted couches and tables.

Gideon hated it.

Ryan and Max weren't here yet, and Gideon's all-black attire was a huge contrast against all the color.

He was thankful it was midweek, slow, and that he didn't have to wait in line with beanied college students. He shoved his hands in his pockets and maneuvered his way to the long L-shaped counter. The barista popped up from a desk on the left hand side, bouncing to the iPad register in the center of the L's short side. He flipped his hair out of his eyes, his smile fading upon making eye contact with Gideon.

The barista looked vaguely familiar, a clouded dream Gideon could barely recall. He cocked his head.

"Do I... know you?"

The barista shook his head. "Not that I know of, but I think I know you. Are you... Gideon?"

Gideon relaxed, smiled. Just a fan.

"Yeah, I am. You like our music?"

The look on the barista's face grew bitter. "Not even a little bit, and I like you even less for what you put Ella through."

Gideon took a step back. "What do you mean? How do you know about me and Ella?"

"How do I know about you and Ella?" the floppy-haired barista scoffed. "Bitch, please. I'm practically her brother. Ben? I know she's mentioned me. You're a dick. You know that, right?" He shook his head.

Ah. Ben. The guy he'd seen Ella with after his AA meeting a few weeks ago.

"I'm sorry about that, I am. But…"

"Hey, Gid." Ryan interrupted him, coming up on his left side while Max was at his right. Their all-black musician outfits were a comfort to Gideon in this very odd place with this very hostile person.

Ben rolled his eyes. "Great, now you're bringing your friends? What can I get you ass wipes?"

"Whoa, there," Ryan said. "We know Gideon's tough, but don't bring us into that." He flashed a smile and Ben softened.

"Fine. I won't serve him. What can I get you two?"

Max laughed while Ryan gave the order, looping Gideon's small black coffee in with their more elaborate flavored lattes. While Ben worked on their drinks, Ryan turned to Gideon.

"Wow, you make an impression. What was that about?"

Gideon shook his head, moving to an empty couch nearby.

"Apparently he's one of Ella's closest friends and he's pissed about everything." He took off his jacket, settling on the loveseat across from the couch where Max took a seat.

"Damn, that's rough. He probably doesn't know you guys are talking," Ryan said before going to get their finished drinks.

"A girl's friends will always hate whoever broke her heart." Max rested his arms on his knees, shaking his head.

Gideon nodded, looking at Ryan leaning on the counter. Ben flipped his hair out of his eyes and smiled at something he said. Ryan gave him a chin nod before turning with all three drinks between his hands. He took a seat beside Max, passing the drinks around, taking a long sip from his iced something or other.

"You can make friends with a brick wall, can't you?" Gideon asked Ryan, eying him over the rim of his cup while Max chuckled.

Ryan shrugged. "Doesn't hurt to be good with people."

"True," Gideon said. "So, guys, what's up?"

Max cleared his throat and leaned back. "I think the three of us — and Lucas, who couldn't make it — have more in common than we think. I want to be friends with you guys, I do. And I'm worried about Anthony."

Anthony was the closest thing Gideon had to a sibling, and he felt himself tense at Max's words.

Gideon was worried about him too but it was usually a brotherly feeling. Having a stranger point out the same thoughts was a new experience, especially since Ryan and Lucas had never said anything about Anthony's substance problems before. He remembered how Anthony had acted at the last band practice and knew his behavior had reached a new level, one that Gideon had been on last year. It was a level that impacted their relationship as a band and as individuals.

"Look, man," Gideon said. "I know you're new here and want to fit in. I get it, I do. I'm also concerned about Ant, but the way you went about the dry tour thing was not the right way. Especially if you want to be together on something? You need to actually talk to everyone instead of blindsiding us."

Max met Gideon's gaze. "Fair enough. I'm sorry you felt blindsided, but as someone who is also trying to maintain a certain lifestyle, I needed to say something."

"Then don't loop other people in with what you want."

The ice in their voices sent a chill through Gideon but he maintained his gaze with Max. At least until Ryan jumped in. "Alright, you two. Max, there are relationships here that need to be considered and Gideon, look at me and tell me you weren't also planning on asking Tom about a dry tour."

Gideon tapped his cup on the coffee table between them, waging a war between his ego and the person he wanted to be. The latter won out. He turned to his friend and ran his hand through his hair.

"I was planning on it, I just wanted to do it privately." He faced Max. "Anthony is prideful. When you call things out, he'll feel attacked. Since Tom is his dad, there was also a level of embarrassment."

Max's eyes grew large, taking Gideon by surprise. "Tom is Anthony's dad?"

Gideon glanced at Ryan, setting his coffee down and leaning forward. "Yeah, man. And I'm Anthony's cousin. You didn't know that?"

He was met with a silent head shake.

"Guess we have a lot to catch you up on," Ryan said.

38

She'd been to Pinewood Rehabilitation Center more times than she could count, but it always threw Ella off standing before the snow white portico. The facility was only about an hour outside of Sugar Grove, tucked away in the mountains, surrounded by tall pines and a gravel drive. Quiet. Peaceful.

Perfect for someone's umpteenth time in recovery.

Ella trudged up the steps, opening the familiar burgundy door to the reception area. The young receptionist looked up and smiled. Her amber hair was pulled into a bun so tight it stretched the skin on her forehead. Ella smiled back.

"Hi, I'm here to see Margaret Davis. My name's Ella Davis, her daughter." She handed over her driver's license.

Bun Lady typed her into the system and, rising, handed her card back. "If you'll just follow me." She led Ella down one of the cream-colored halls to a small room in the back that served for family visits. The young woman left to get Margaret. Ella sat at a round table by one of the tall windows and looked out over the lawn. Some of the other inpatients were outside, sitting and walking around.

"Ms. Davis?"

The receptionist startled Ella, and it took her a moment to realize she hadn't returned with her mom.

"I'm sorry, but your mother says she didn't approve your visit."

Ella stared at her.

"What do you mean? I'm her daughter, I haven't seen her in almost three months."

"I'm really sorry, there's nothing I can do."

Ella looked to the open door, hoping Margaret would glide on through, give her the smile only a mom could give her child.

"Ms. Davis? I'm really sorry, but I'm going to have to escort you back to the lobby."

Ella turned her attention to Bun Lady, a weight settling over her shoulders. She felt tired. Depleted.

"Should've expected it. You can have her call

me." Ella stormed past the receptionist, her purse accidentally hitting the woman on the way out. The cream colored walls merged together, the lobby a mesh of colors as she flung open the door to freedom. She stumbled over blurred gravel and fallen leaves to her car. Leaning against the driver's side door, she let the tears spill over. Even after all this time, she'd hoped things would be different. That her mom would want her daughter as badly as Ella wanted her mom.

It never got old.

Ella fumbled with the car door, sliding in away from the fall chill. Sitting felt nice. Solid. She calmed herself, slowed the heaving and trembling, gripped the steering wheel with both hands. Control. She was in control. She took a few deep breaths and wiped her eyes, her sight clearing. Ella knew there was nothing to be done but to wait for her mom's call. It was a game she was used to. She knew her mom was in good hands, and Ella needed to focus on moving to New York City.

And on Gideon.

Shame and vulnerability had kept her from sharing her mom with him, but eventually she'd have to push through it. He deserved to know, and relationships were built on trust. Especially if they were going to try their relationship again, for real, she needed to open herself to him. Ella knew Gideon would never judge her, but she was terrified of him hurting her again. She took several deep breaths, trying to force down the anxiety in her chest. She started the car, easing her way down the long drive. She didn't want to be alone, but she didn't want people. She didn't want pity or questions; she wanted to be held and comforted.

39

Gideon hadn't been to Anthony's apartment in God knew how long.

His cousin also hadn't invited Gideon and wasn't aware of the impending visit.

The building was closer to Sugar Grove than Gideon's and on a busy street. He had walked the twenty or so minutes, inviting the brisk air to calm his mind. After the meeting with Ryan and Max, Gideon had realized it'd been awhile since he and Anthony had spent time alone. The flask incident last year had impacted their relationship and, while they were able to party and have fun on tour, once Gideon went into recovery they had grown apart. He recognized Anthony's declining behavior as his own and wanted to be the friend he hadn't had.

He sounded the buzzer for the third time, stepping out from under the overhang to look up to the fifth floor where Anthony lived. It was possible he was still sleeping, but Gideon hadn't wanted to risk his cousin having "plans" in an effort to avoid him.

He pressed the button again, holding it this time for effect.

When he released it, the buzz for unlocking the doors answered back.

The stairs were steep and slippery — new — and a slick elevator hid behind them. Gideon waited for the hushed machine to take him to the fifth floor, looking at his many reflections in the mirrored walls. The elevator halted smoothly, opening to a carpeted hallway. He sank with each step, stopping in front of Anthony's door. He'd rehearsed what he was going to say over and over again but still didn't feel prepared.

Gideon rapped on the door and it pushed open. He stepped through, his cousin a disheveled heap on the beat-up couch he'd had since college. There was a musty odor clinging to the air as Gideon closed the door behind him, Anthony eyeing him through half-closed lids.

"What are you doing here, man?"

"Wanted to check up on you, it's been awhile," Gideon said, making his way past the couch to the kitchen situated on the wall opposite the door. The counters were covered in something sticky and a pizza box with a slice left inside. Lime remnants sat in the sink beside several beer bottles and one vodka handle. "You doing okay?" He looked back to the couch. Anthony was sitting up, running his hand through his black hair. He grumbled something before shuffling over to Gideon.

"Yeah, I'm great. Want a hair of the dog with me?" He leaned on the peninsula that acted as a divide between the kitchen and the living room.

Gideon looked at him. "Dude... I'm sober."

Anthony returned his stare, taking a moment before the realization hit him.

"Shit, sorry. Guess just one for me." He opened the fridge while Gideon wiped the counters. Gideon tossed the pizza, watching his friend make a drink.

"Hey, man. That's actually something I wanted to ask you about." The words slipped out and Gideon busied himself with the items in the sink, waiting for Anthony's reaction.

The fridge opened and slammed shut, followed by a long slurp and a bang on the counter.

"Seriously? You gonna come at me with this shit, too?"

Gideon recognized the defensiveness. He'd given

Tom a similar attitude. He dried his hand on one of the dishtowels hanging from the stove before turning to face his cousin.

"Ant, I've been there. You know that."

They stared off. Anthony downed his drink, never breaking eye contact. He set the glass down hard before heading back to the couch. Gideon moved the empty glass into the sink before tailing him.

"I'm one to party, you know that," Gideon said. "But tell me I'm wrong when I say this has gone past partying."

He brushed crumbs off one of the depressed couch cushions before taking a seat. Turning to Anthony, he watched his friend hang his head and sigh. They sat in silence, Gideon wanting to give him space.

"It's just so hard, man." Anthony looked up, and Gideon watched his eyes turn glassy. "I honestly don't know how you do it."

Gideon leaned back. "I do it because I have to." Thoughts of Ella raced through his mind, how she'd helped him see the light at the end of the tunnel. How she'd helped him find a sense of purpose. "I know the life I want, and alcohol doesn't fit with that."

"But how do you just... stop?" His head dropped into his hands. "I enjoy it. I feel good. Like people are actually seeing me."

The words could have been taken straight out of Gideon's own mind. He loved the sense of freedom drinking gave him, like he just didn't have to think for once. He was lucky to have found practices like meditation that delivered a similar result, but he knew the sense of being liked was stronger with a vice.

He also knew needing to be liked was driven by ego, and that was a core issue Anthony would have to work on.

Gideon looked at his cousin in his moment of despair, knowing the road he had ahead of him. He thought of his own journey, how he'd been saved time and time again. How grateful he was to be able to see things more clearly than before.

He had found — built — a life he loved, and Anthony needed the same.

As his friend, his family, Gideon would do everything in his power to help.

40

"As you can see, the space is perfect for up to fifteen employees. And you can't beat the view!" Their real estate agent Oliver played Vanna White, his pageantry flowing in full force. It was the fourth office space he'd shown them, but the only one that felt warm despite its size.

Rachel's heels clacked to the windows taking up the whole back wall while Ella turned in a circle, feeling small in the generous space. Her Ked's were muffled on the light laminate flooring as she walked toward Rachel. There was a kitchenette on the wall next to the windows. And Oliver was right — Maven Media could easily entertain clients and grow their company in this space. It was large, warm.

It reminded Ella of one of the group activity rooms at Pinewood Rehab. She tried to push thoughts of her mom out of her head but knew she couldn't stop the slow breaking of her heart. Every now and then, Margaret would remove her status as "mom." She'd cut and run from Ella's life for periods of time, forcing Ella to get used to being on her own. Right when she started navigating life by herself, her mom would come back into the picture. Margaret would be "ready" to resume her responsibilities. And Ella would fall right back into their old relationship, as if nothing had changed.

Ella trailed her fingers over the kitchen counters on her way to stand beside Rachel. The windows overlooked the East River in New York City, a prime office location in the Brooklyn neighborhood of Dumbo. Sitting between the Brooklyn Bridge and the Manhattan Bridge, the occasional rumble of subways could be heard. It was a sort of white noise, one that was simultaneously comforting and foreign. Rachel folded her arms over her navy wool coat, beaming.

"This is it. Can't you feel it?" Her high ponytail swung when she turned to face Ella. "I think we have to take it, they're offering a discount if we sign a three year lease."

Ella looked at Rachel. "But aren't most businesses in Manhattan? Shouldn't we try to be there?"

"Why would we try to be where everyone else is when we could be one of the first somewhere else?"

She had a point. Ella shuffled her feet, feeling less competent beside her partner. Expecting to hike around NYC, she'd opted for tennis shoes and jeans. Rachel had opted for the opposite, and her confidence showed. She crossed over to Oliver, who had stayed towards the door, dressed in a navy suit and black peacoat that was a sharp contrast to the white walls.

Ella wanted to have the authority that radiated off Rachel. Ella was better about standing up for what she wanted than she was last year, but there was always room from growth. She wanted change. She gave one last look out the window, enjoying the glitter of the river and the rumble of the trains, before joining her two laughing companions.

"This is beautiful, Oliver. Thank you for showing us," Ella said.

He smiled between the two of them. "It's my pleasure. I probably would've failed college if it wasn't for Rachel. She doesn't play around when it comes to business."

Ella laughed, knowing full-well what he meant.

"Oh, stop." Rachel swatted his arm, her eyes

betraying her affection for him. "I needed a study buddy as badly as you did."

They talked about the potential layout for desks and tables before heading out into the bracing air. The wind off the river was intense, and Ella huddled under her thrifted faux fur coat while trailing behind Oliver and Rachel. The two old friends laughed and talked almost the entire time while they waited for the car to pick them up and take them to Oliver's office. Ella couldn't help but smile. She rarely saw Rachel relaxed, let alone flirting.

The ride from Brooklyn to Manhattan was long thanks to traffic, and when they finally arrived at the office in the Flatiron District, they all did some variation of a stumble out of the car. It never failed to amaze Ella how, in the City, it could take forty minutes to drive a few miles. They entered a building across from the famous Flatiron building, taking the elevator to the real estate office Oliver worked at. The modern office belonged in a magazine, and so did the people that worked there. They reached his office and he shut the door, taking a seat behind his desk while they settled in the armchairs facing him.

"So, ladies, did you have a favorite?" He leaned back in his chair, folding his hands across his stomach. He smiled at them both, but his gaze held on Rachel. She sat at the edge of her chair, ankles crossed, a smile still plastered to her face, and turned to face Ella.

"I think so. Right, El?"

Ella nodded, her voice lost. An age-old dream of being in a big city, making a name for herself, was actually coming true. Her mom would be ecstatic. At least she would be once she spoke to Ella again. The burn of not being able to share this good news with her mom sat with Ella, the heat rising to her face. She blinked her eyes to clear away any potential tears and looked at her partner, her friend. Rachel smiled at her and turned back to Oliver, hands animated and the Dumbo location on her lips. Oliver pulled out a folder while they discussed the lease and next steps, highlighting the documents.

They were doing this.

41

Gideon took his time walking down the long hallway that led to the recording booth, his guitar heavy on his back. Him and Anthony had a great heart-to-heart yesterday. His cousin had broke down, still tipsy from the night before and already getting started that morning, going over things from not fitting in in high school to the divorce of his parents and the estrangement of his mom. Gideon had had no idea Anthony was holding onto these things; all he'd been able to do was sit and listen. After Anthony had exhausted himself, they'd agreed on getting him into a program, and Gideon had left feeling lighter about the direction of his family and the band.

But this would be the first time seeing his cousin since that talk. The last time Anthony didn't drink during band practice had been before their tour with The National, when the band had supported Gideon being sober by joining him. It had lasted two weeks before Anthony showed up to a show with a flask. And that's just what Gideon had seen; he had no way of knowing whether or not Anthony had actually been sober those two weeks when he wasn't with the band.

The door was ajar, and he saw Tom and Nate, the label rep, sitting with the producer and sound engineer. The rest of the band was already on the other side of the glass, standing in a circle talking.

Tom looked up as Gideon entered and threw him a small smile. "Hey, Gid. We're just going over some of the sax adjustments. Why don't you hop in there and we can get started?"

"Yeah, sure thing," Gideon said, nodding hello to the other men before joining his bandmates.

The band was discussing which song they wanted to start with. Anthony was sulking, arms crossed while the other three agreed on the order — *Panic, Open, Dahlia*. He glanced at Gideon but didn't say anything. Lucas started tapping out the beat to the first song while Ryan adjusted his bass, Max blowing softly into his sax. Anthony picked up his guitar, avoiding all eye contact with the band.

Gideon slung his guitar around his neck and tuned the instrument to the song. He started playing the opening, his mates following suit. They needed to warm up before he started singing. Anthony plucked at his strings but was missing the energy he usually brought with him. Gideon tried to make eye contact with him, not wanting to call him out, but his cousin stared at the floor.

"Hey guys?" Tom's voice come over the intercom.

Everyone stopped playing, looking through the window.

"I know it's a warm-up but we need a little more oomph. Why don't we run through the song a couple times, no pressure, and then we'll record?"

Gideon nodded, turning to face Ryan and Lucas. Anthony stayed on his left and Max moved in between Anthony and Lucas to close the circle. Lucas counted to four before launching into *Panic*, one of the very first songs the band had ever written. Gideon sang, his baritone carrying a hint of middle school emo reminiscent of his favorite pop punk bands. They'd played the song hundreds of times and had rehearsed with Max dozens of times, but the sax still felt foreign to Gideon when it joined. Discordant.

Finishing the song, the band looked to the men

behind the window. Nate was saying something to Tom, the sound engineer nodding and adjusting his board. Gideon didn't need them to say anything; something was off.

He sighed, turning back to his friends.

"I guess let's try that again. Max, that was good, the sax feels weird but in a good way," Gideon said.

"It's very... panicky, right?" Max laughed at his own joke, causing everyone to smile. Everyone but Anthony.

"Yo, man, you good?" Gideon asked him.

"Yeah, let's just fucking finish this." Anthony turned away from the group, playing his part. Gideon looked at the others, their faces betraying the worry they felt. Anthony had always had an attitude, but it was usually balanced with a joke or a smile. This was just... angry.

Lucas tapped four beats before they launched into the song. The flow felt a tad better than before, the sax merging with the other instruments more seamlessly. When they got to the second verse Anthony stopped playing. Dumbfounded, the band kept playing, dropping off as they watched Anthony remove his guitar and stomp from the room.

"Hey, man, where you going?" Ryan called out to Anthony's retreating back.

Gideon watched Tom run from the room, Nate dropping his head in his hands. The producer and sound engineer shook their heads before standing, stretching, and leaving the booth. Gideon faced his mates, the silence stretching between them. Anthony had never acted like that, and no one knew how to react.

Ryan sighed, leaning his bass against the wall. He crossed his arms over his chest. "Well." Lucas stood, setting his sticks on his snare. He looked at the guys. "I've never seen that before."

Gideon chewed his lower lip. "Me neither, but I think I know why."

He launched into a recap of the conversation he and Anthony had had yesterday, sticking to the reliance on alcohol and Anthony's desire to change while avoiding the more personal information Anthony had shared. The guys listened while he spoke, and when he finished they just stared at him.

"So..." Ryan began. "He's been sober for a day? That's why he's acting like a dick?"

Lucas shook his head. "That's nuts. But what about last year, when we were all sober for a couple weeks?"

"You really think he was sober then?" Max chimed in.

Gideon looked at their new bandmate. Max would understand more than anyone else how removing a dependency could alter a person, and he'd voiced the same concerns Gideon had walking into the room. Anthony had never stormed out of a band practice, let alone a recording studio.

They looked up as Tom came into the room.

"Okay," he said, sighing. He placed his hands on his hips, looking at each member. "He left. We need to reschedule."

"What?" They said it unison.

Tom just stood there, nodding his head. "Yep. I... Yep. He left. I'm going to see if we can get recording time Monday but we'll meet at the rehearsal room first. 10 a.m. Sound good?"

He was relatively calm, but Gideon knew his uncle well enough to see the cracks below the surface. Tom was pissed, upset, disappointed.

"Guys, we good?" His voice cracked.

They nodded their heads, murmuring in agreement to the time. Tom nodded and went to the recording booth to give the news. Gideon looked at his friends, everyone standing in a state of shock.

Muffled yelling came from behind the window, and they turned to look. Nate, the label rep, was animated, Tom hanging his head. Nate stormed past their manager. Tom raised his head, looking at what was left of Eternal Youths. He nodded and walked out, leaving the band in the recording space.

"I guess... I guess I'll see you Monday." Gideon knew he'd spoken, but the words felt disconnected from himself. He saw more than felt himself repack his guitar, the weight on his back heavier than before. He watched the other members pack up their things, their conversation ranging from concerned to angry as they went over what Anthony had done. How it could ruin their chances with their label, 4AD, one of the biggest in the industry.

Gideon left before them, wanting to be alone. He needed a drink, which meant he needed a meeting.

42

The contract revisions stared at Ella from her desk, Julie and Rachel's voices breaking into her thoughts of the impending phone call with Charlie at Blue Bird Books. She glanced at the clock, trying to tamp down her anxiety.

T-minus fifteen minutes.

Ella stood, gathering the documents and walking to the loveseat where her two best friends sat discussing the changes Julie had made. Julie was on her way to becoming a lawyer, studying for the bar exam and working as a paralegal, so she offered her knowledge and connections when she could. Ella set the papers on the coffee table, sitting in an armchair across from them.

"Alrighty, I'm excited. I think this will be it. How

do you feel, Ella?" Rachel turned her espresso eyes to her.

"I feel good about it, too. She should be fine with the changes Julie made, they're so minor but we need to make sure everyone is working on an agreeable timeline with enough notice for certain projects." Ella watched Julie pick up the pages, flipping through them one last time.

Rachel nodded. "Agreed. Also, I have a meeting with Jen from Bonnier Books next week. She wants to look into contracting us once we get settled in the city." She leaned back, adjusting her blazer. Her silk trousers shone with the overhead light as she shook her leg.

Rachel didn't get nervous. At least not from what Ella had seen.

They'd signed the lease on the office space in Dumbo but they needed Blue Bird Books in order to actually afford it. They'd narrowly missed losing the account on their last phone call with Charlie but until the money showed up, the account wasn't theirs.

Julie passed the papers back to Ella and checked her watch.

"Okay, ladies, we got this! And after, could we please go celebrate with happy hour drinks? It's been a long week," Julie said, adjusting her dress while Rachel pulled out her phone to make the call.

The phone sat on the coffee table, ringing on speaker while they waited for Charlie to pick up.

"Hi Rachel, how are you?" Charlie's low voice came through.

"We're good Charlie, thank you. I have Ella and Julie, our legal rep, with me." Rachel leaned forward, holding her hand out to Ella for the contract.

"Perfect, we're joined on my end by our legal team and my assistant, Cormack." They heard shuffling on the other end. "We approve the changes, but I wanted to ask if we could put in a trial end date."

Ella looked at Rachel and Julie.

"Hi Charlie, this is Julie. What would the terms be?"

More shuffling. "My team says we can add a clause to page ten, under section F in regards to the one year renewal. I'd like to have a month-to-month trial period for the first six months with the ability to cancel the contract with thirty days notice."

Ella stared at Rachel, miming to put Charlie on mute.

"That shouldn't be an issue but let me briefly put you on hold while we discuss," Rachel said, trying to mask the confusion in her voice with a smile. Charlie agreed and Rachel pressed the mute button.

"What the fuck." Ella bit her lower lip. "Why would they want a trial period?"

"Well, it is a lot of money. It's not uncommon, I just wish she'd said something sooner," Julie piped in. She took the contract from Rachel, flipping to page ten. "It's a relatively easy addition, I'll just have to add it and they'll have to approve it."

"What does that do for our timeline? We need to lock this down." Rachel's voice was icy.

Julie sighed. "It depends on how long they take, I can fix the clause after the call. But you said they want to get this situated, right? So my guess is by middle of next week."

"Fine." Rachel turned the mute off.

Ella jumped in before Rachel could take over. "Hi Charlie, it's Ella. That's not a problem, we can have the revised contract sent this evening with the appropriate changes." She needed to prove she was as much a partner as Rachel, and there was a sinking feeling in her stomach that Charlie wanted the month-to-month clause because she didn't trust Maven Media. Because she didn't trust Ella.

"That works." Charlie didn't try to hide the distaste in her voice. "We'll review tonight and send either the adjusted or the signed version to you on Monday. I look forward to meeting in person once you guys are settled in the city."

"Likewise. Thanks so much, Charlie." They signed off, ending the call.

Julie stood and stretched, moving to her bag resting against Ella's desk. "Wow, pissy much? Like, I know you bumbled the first call but can't she just let it go?"

Rachel shook her head. "I really don't understand, but at least she's signing. We have to figure out movers after we sign, once that first payment comes through."

Ella looked at her partner, the timeline sinking in. "We also need to figure out apartments. It sounds like we'll be moving in the next couple weeks."

"My family has an apartment in the Upper West Side, we can stay there for the time being while we get our feet under us. My dad sometimes stays there for business, but it's got five bedrooms. I'll talk to him. And then we don't have to deal with paying rent." Rachel stood, smoothing her pants and strutting to her desk where Julie sat working on her laptop. Ella watched them. They were the family she'd created, and there was no one else Ella would rather build a business or live with.

Except Gideon.

Her heart ached for his touch. They had plans to see each other tomorrow, but it couldn't come fast enough. She missed the way he smelled, the sound of his voice, the way he held her. She knew he would eventually move to the city, but her plans were coming up more quickly than his. His plan was barely thought up. She didn't know how they'd fare with the distance, especially since there was no visible end date.

"Sent." Julie's voice cut through her thoughts, and Ella stood to grab her bag. It was five o'clock somewhere, and she didn't want to think about anything that could keep her from Gideon.

43

The folding chairs never seemed to get comfortable, no matter how many times Gideon sat in them or for how long. He half-listened to someone finishing up their story for the week, his sponsor Amy listening beside him with rapt attention. The room clapped as the guy left the front of the room, Gideon having missed most of what he said. He shifted in his seat, his leg bouncing. His hand played with his green chip, wishing it was a glass tumbler. It'd been over an hour. He'd gotten there early, hoping to catch Amy before the meeting started, but she'd arrived just as the meeting began. Gideon had planted himself in his chair, people-watching the packed room. Fridays always had a large crowd.

"Hey Gideon, you're not gonna share?"

Gideon blinked, turning to Amy. She'd whispered, leaning towards him, her curly hair brushing his shoulder. The meeting leader, Joseph, stood at the front of the room, asking if there was anyone else who wanted to share.

"Nah, I actually wanted to talk to you," he whispered back.

Her lips quirked into a sympathetic smile and she patted his arm, turning back to the front. No one else raised their hand. Joesph pointed to the refreshments and thanked everyone for coming.

"Thank fucking god." Gideon stood, shaking out his legs. Amy joined him. She was all of five feet, her baby face almost always carrying a smile. Including now, her hand outstretched, holding his coat.

"Aw, it wasn't that bad. C'mon, let's grab some coffee and you can tell me what's going on. We haven't talked in awhile."

Amy scooted out of the row of chairs, taking her time to greet those she knew and smile at the ones she didn't. She'd been in the program for over two years and regularly offered to help people when they needed it. Gideon followed, his long legs tripping over the people still seated. Most everyone was standing, mingling, laughing. Gideon fingered the green chip in his pocket.

They made their way to the refreshments table,

Amy grabbing two styrofoam cups and filling them with coffee. It was weak, but it was free. Gideon sipped the steaming liquid as they crossed to an empty corner. Amy turned to face him, leaning against the wall and pushing her glasses up the bridge of her nose.

"Talk to me, Pike." Her calling him by his last name made him smile. She meant business, even if she was being playful.

Gideon let out a long breath. He'd played through the conversation in his head, but there were a lot of things Amy would have a comment for. He decided to start with Ella. He told Amy they were back together and about his plans to propose. Amy's face never changed; she just listened to him and sipped her coffee.

"There's no real rule against relationships when you're in the program, but you and I both know it's smarter to hold off," she said after he'd finished. "The hardest part about dating when you're in this thing is making sure you don't replace one vice with another." She cocked her head, her dark eyes staring into his.

He nodded, looking away. "I know. Last time I'd made my recovery about her. This time it's about me, and the life I want. She makes me want to be the best man I can be. I lost her once, and I can't risk losing her again."

Amy sighed. "Okay. Look, only you know what's best for you. But having been in your position before — and having the added peer pressure from working in the music business — just promise me you'll be careful, okay?"

He nodded. "There's another thing."

Gideon turned to face her, launching into telling her about his conversation with Anthony and how the recording day had devolved. His throat felt choked, face heated by the time he stopped.

"Oh, Gideon. You know he's where you were a few months ago. He's struggling, and you know what that feels like. The problem is, he's family. He's your cousin and your co-worker. But he's the same one that pulled you back to your old life last year. And you can't risk that again."

"I know that. He won't."

"Pike, you don't know that." She rested her hand on his shoulder. "You may need to create more distance between you two. I know he needs help, but that's not your responsibility. Not while you're still recovering."

"Ames, I can't just leave him." His heart clenched, fear coursing through his body at what would happen to Anthony if Gideon wasn't there for him.

"I'm not saying that. But part of recovering is understanding not just bad habits and triggers, but recognizing the people that could push us back to where we're trying to leave. And he's not alone. You said his dad is very involved, right?" She looked up at him, cocking her head.

"Yeah." Gideon thought of how Tom had pulled him aside, asking him to keep an eye out. How Tom tried to hide his hurt, his disappointment, at his son behaving the way he did.

"Okay. So it's not your job. We have to do what's best for us, and you can't help anyone if you're not helping yourself first."

Gideon looked at her. Her face had softened, the hint of a smile still there. "I'm sorry, Gideon. It sucks and it's hard but that's how it is. I know you. You're strong, and you know what's right. I trust you, and I think you need to trust yourself."

He nodded. She was right. He replayed the conversation he'd had with Anthony. His cousin really seemed ready to change, but the first couple of weeks were the hardest. Everything was in technicolor, noises at volumes you never knew existed. Gideon sighed. Anthony was probably just feeling overwhelmed and band practice was the last thing he wanted to deal with.

"Thanks, Amy." He bent down to give her a one-armed hug.

"C'mon, let's go grab some cookies before they're gone. If we can't drink we might as well eat!" She laughed her way to the table, Gideon following.

If he couldn't drink, he might as well eat.

44

Meow.

Meow.

Ella struggled to open her eyes, her head pounding like a drum. Pollack sat at the foot of her bed, insistent she wake up and feed him. She tightened the covers around her.

Meow.

"Fine, fine," she grumbled, aching as she rose from the comfy bed. Ella padded down the hall, the chilly air a shock to her system despite being wrapped in a blanket she'd stolen from the bed. She guzzled some water, scooping the wet food for Pollack while waiting for the coffee to brew. Her favorite mug was soon filled with the magical elixir. She carried it to the couch with her phone and crawled under her blanket.

After the call with Charlie, Julie had sent the adjusted contract. They'd gone out for happy hour at Gooseberry, a cute bar new to Sugar Grove and a few blocks from their office. Rachel had enjoyed vodka martinis, Julie had her standard gin and tonic, and Ella had indulged in her personal favorite: margaritas. They'd then hopped to O'Brien's and stayed out way later than planned. Ella's old stomping ground hadn't changed in the year since she quit as one of their bartenders. Frat boys and sorority girls lined the walls or huddled around the two pool tables, talking or dancing or making out. The girls had found a spot by the bar and stayed there most of the night, talking and drinking. A couple guys had come over to flirt with them until Rachel put on her business demeanor and dismissed them from their girl's night. They didn't end up parting until the first light of sunrise peeked over the horizon.

Ella checked her social medias and her email before shooting Gideon a good morning text. She was seeing him that night and couldn't ignore the butterflies in her stomach. Or the fact that he still gave her butterflies. Warmth spread through her body at the thought of him, and she wished he was nestled behind her, wrapping his long limbs around her beneath the blanket.

Pollack jumped onto her legs, resting between her legs and cleaning himself.

"Seriously?" she asked. He stopped and looked at her before resuming his task. Fucking cats. But she'd never do anything to disrupt him. She went back to her phone.

Nothing from Gideon.

Nothing from her mom.

Ella sighed, feeling apathetic. It was that feeling of having so much to do that procrastination was the only obvious answer. She really needed to start figuring out the move. The office lease started November 1st and it was already midway through October. Ella had about two weeks to sort her life and figure out which boxes she'd take with her and which ones she'd be leaving behind.

She rose, not moving her legs. Her head still hurt, but the coffee had helped. Carefully working around Pollack, she got up from the couch. Ella made her way to the bookshelf by the window and kneeled before it. The shelves held her prized possessions — books, photos, sentimental trinkets. A cheap black frame with an aged photo stared at her, and she fingered the handsome man in the image. He held her, an infant, both smiling with the joy only a baby could bring. It was her only picture of the man.

He and her mom had relied on each other, which only ended in a very dramatic, very public custody battle when she was a toddler. Afterwards, James Berry, the famous actor, her father, had gone down the rehab rabbit hole. He'd been one of the leading actors of his generation until he got even further sidetracked with parties and the newfound freedom of divorce. Ella had heard the stories. She'd watched his movies, read scores of news articles, watched interviews, seen his slow demise through others' eyes. The one thing she didn't have was contact with him. It had been part of the custody arrangement, as he was seen to be unfit, and when she'd turned eighteen her mom had begged Ella to not reach out to him, citing that he would find her and take anything worth taking. So she hadn't reached out.

Ella picked up the frame, tracing the man. Eventually, her research had resulted in a dead end. James Berry had disappeared from the public eye, and no one cared enough to find him. She set the frame beside her, picking up its sister frame. Her mom's eyes stared back, young, Ella a laughing toddler beside her. This was the Margaret she remembered. This was the Margaret she saw when her mom laughed. And when her mom sounded small. Ella sighed, placing it on top of the first frame. She started pulling books from the shelves, taking her time with each one while she decided which ones were worth the weight to move.

When she finally had two clear piles of keep and let go, she checked the time. After sorting through so many memories, she felt more tired than when she'd woken up. Ella hopped up to take a quick shower and pull herself together. Gideon would be there in a couple hours to pick her up. She wanted — needed — to look and feel her best.

45

Gideon had never before been surrounded by so many diamonds.

The foyer of the jewelry store was chilly but warmer than outside, and Julie was running late. He'd reached out to her on Instagram, doing his best to explain why he deserved another, more final chance with her best friend. Julie had been cold, but he couldn't blame her. She'd eventually come around and promised to help him find the perfect ring.

Gideon's hands were in his pocket, playing with his newly earned purple chip. Amy had helped him with the Anthony situation, and they'd eaten cookies and drunk coffee with a few of the other members that didn't want the Friday night reminder of what they were missing. Until that night he'd been shit with communicating with Amy, having been distracted with Ella and the band. But confiding in Amy had lifted a weight he hadn't realized he'd been holding. He felt good. Strong.

It was a relief, talking to everyone and no one, these strangers who were also his friends. And it was a nice reminder for why he'd started going to the meetings in the first place. Amy had given him the chip when they parted and it had taken the place of his green one. Green had reminded him of Ella's eyes. Purple was the color of royalty, and Ella was his queen.

"You're lucky she likes you so much." Julie's voice matched his icy surroundings. He turned to face her. She could be Ella's sister with how much they resembled one another. Her long blonde hair tumbled out of a raspberry knit cap, arctic eyes shooting flames. She looked tired, and her face was beat red from the cold outside.

"Believe me, I know. Thanks so much for coming, I want to get this right and no one knows her like you do." Gideon shuffled under her scrutiny.

She sighed. "I mean, you're not wrong. I want her to be happy and you seem to be doing the work you need to do on yourself. But..." She glared at him.

"You fucking hurt her again and you're dead. Are we clear?"

"Absolutely."

"Okay. She's simple but classy and she likes old things. I say we look around, I'll show you what I think she'll like and you say yay or nay. But honestly, Gideon? I would take these ideas and find something vintage for her." She brushed past him, the first case catching her eye. He followed and, stopping beside her, looked at the rings before him.

They all looked the same.

"I like this one," Julie said, tapping the glass above a rather large ring. "What do you think?"

An attendant came over at her request and removed the ring, handing it to Gideon. Julie leaned in to look at it while Gideon turned it over in his hands.

"When's the special day?"

Both of them snapped their heads to look at the attendant. His oblivious smile grew painful when they glanced at one another.

"Over my dead body," Julie huffed. "It's for my best friend." She took the ring from Gideon, trying it on her finger. The attendant mumbled an apology before regaining composure and going on about the ring specs. Gideon could only stare at the large rock on the band filled with diamonds encircling Julie's finger, trying to imagine it on Ella.

Gideon shook his head. "Too flashy."

Julie looked at him over her shoulder, sighed, and placed it back on the counter. She moved to the next case, also filled with rings that felt too flashy. Julie pulled another one out, a large square surrounded by smaller stones.

"She's not really a square person to me, Julie." Gideon took the ring from her. "What about something simple, like a gold band and a really pretty single stone?"

"You mean... a solitaire ring?" She smirked.

He rolled his eyes. "Sure. You know what I mean though, right?"

"Sure. What about something like this, a halo?" She pointed to another large diamond, this one surrounded by a circle of smaller ones. "Or maybe something old-fashioned, like that?" She pointed to a teardrop-shaped stone.

Gideon chewed his lower lip, contemplating what fit Ella best. He had saved most of the money from tour and had saved a fortune from not drinking. A large diamond would do Ella justice, but he knew she'd want something with a story. Something that had a history, like she did. Like they did.

"Gideon?"

He looked at Julie, her face tilted towards his. She gave a small smile and placed her hand on his arm. "I do support this, I promise. Hard for me to not be protective over my best friend, especially after everything she's been through."

He nodded. "I get it, I do. So... Solitaire, halo, or maybe the teardrop?"

"You mean pear?" She chuckled. "Yeah, those sound good. C'mon, I brought my laptop. Let's go to The Lava Java and check out our vintage options."

Gideon checked his phone. He still had a few hours before picking up Ella for dinner, and the sooner he researched rings, the sooner he could propose.

46

Ella looked in the full-length mirror one last time, smoothing her dress. The silver sequins were arranged in an art deco pattern over black, the thin straps showing off her collarbone. She slipped on her black satin stilettos and smoothed her straightened hair one last time. Gideon had only said he was taking her to dinner, but she was already looking forward to dessert.

A knock on her front door caused her to jump. She always forgot her building's front door was sticky but never locked. Ella grabbed her purse from the bed and walked to her apartment door, flinging it open. And damn, had the view never looked so good.

Gideon Pike leaned against the doorjamb in a suit.

A suit.

Her rockstar boyfriend knew how to clean up. She'd only ever seen him in jeans and an array of T-shirts or the occasional button-down. His broad shoulders were now encased in a sharp jacket, a black silk tie popping against the crisp white of his shirt. His hands were in his pockets. She did a once-over before resting on his face, where he wore a wicked grin and his hair fell in his eyes.

"Damn." His voice came out as a whisper, one hand reaching for hers.

"You're one to talk, sir," she whispered back. His eyes took on a heat normally reserved for the bedroom. His hand was rough in hers and she pulled him into her entryway.

"You remember what I said about that, right?" He gazed at her behind lowered lids, his tongue slowly licking his bottom lip. Ella pressed herself against him, her heels bringing her closer to his mouth. He was a wall of muscle against her. She ran her hands along his arms, felt his biceps below the fabric, how they flexed when he wrapped his arms around her. He dove in for a kiss and Ella forgot everything outside of his body against hers, the way his mouth claimed hers.

His hands gripped her ass, pulling her tight

against his hard cock. Ella whimpered, her hands finding their way to his waistband. Gideon broke from the kiss, chuckling, panting.

"You know I want nothing more than to feel your naked body against mine, but we do have a reservation." He lifted one of her hands to his lips, kissing the top while staring at her through hooded eyes.

A smolder.

That's the only way to describe how he looked at her, and Ella felt herself swoon. She sighed, resting her hand on the back of his neck.

"Fine," she said, her hand moving to the top of his head. "But I need you to make it up to me later." Her hands twined in his hair and pulled, her lips finding their way to his neck. She nipped and soothed the bite with a kiss. He groaned, his hands squeezing her hips.

"As you wish."

Ella pulled away and looked at him. He'd used her favorite movie line when he had showed up at her office. They'd come so far in the past month. She smiled and kissed him on the cheek before throwing on her winter coat.

Gideon had parked in front of her building but he offered his arm for the walk to the passenger side door, opening it for her with a squeak and closing it after she folded her legs in. She hadn't been in his car since he rescued her from the cupcake shop. When she'd realized she was never going to get what she wanted if she didn't learn how to open herself. That that was the same qualm she had with Gideon but she'd had that problem too.

He jumped in, clicking his seat belt and looking at her with a wide grin.

"You ready for this?"

Ella laughed at his enthusiasm, her earlier melancholy disappearing briefly.

"With you? Always."

47

Gideon couldn't stop smiling as he drove them from the village of Sugar Grove to the bigger city of Poughkeepsie. They rarely left Sugar Grove — it was a walking town, a college town, and had at least one of everything. There never seemed to be a reason to leave. But Gideon wanted to treat Ella to something special. She'd been working hard, and he knew she was at least a little stressed about the impending move.

They'd started the drive in good spirits, throwing on one of Gideon's Spotify playlists. But eventually their excited chatter and Ella's repeated, "Where are we going?" gave way to silence. Gideon glanced over occasionally only to find her staring out the window or biting her lip.

"Darlin', what's on your mind?"

Damnit. He couldn't stop himself. He didn't want to ruin the night, but she was clearly preoccupied with something.

"Nothing." She gave him a weak smile before turning back to the window.

"El, c'mon." He kept his eyes on the highway but saw in his periphery the slump in her shoulders.

She took a deep breath. "Just the moving thing and work. And some stuff with my mom. I'm tired, is all."

"I'm sorry." Gideon kept his eyes forward. She gave him a perfect opportunity to ask more about her mom but he didn't want her to feel like he was going to make a big deal about it. He waited for her to continue and, when she didn't, he took his chance.

"How is your mom? She still in rehab?" Gideon held his breath.

"Yep." Ella's tone was emotionless, stony. Gideon felt himself bordering on desperate, wanting her to open to him like he'd done for her so many times. Wanting her to feel comfortable enough with him that she could.

"Ella, please talk to me."

She turned to the window. "We signed on an office space and are moving to the city in about two weeks. I went to see her the other day, my mom, and she didn't want to see me. I haven't heard from her. And I don't know what to do about her. Or about you."

Gideon's heart lurched. He knew they'd gone to look at offices, but she hadn't told him they'd actually signed on one. He processed what she'd said, trying to find a place to start.

"Okay. First thing's first. What do you mean you don't know what to do about me?"

Ella sighed. "I mean, I'm leaving in two weeks and I... I'm scared we won't be able to do the distance. And you don't really have a plan to move yet."

"Ella, I'll go back and forth if I have to, but my mom still lives there. We've been talking on the phone every week, I'm sure she'd love it if I moved back. Even if it's only for a few days each week while I find an apartment. Please don't worry about that, we'll figure it out. We always do." Gideon took an exit off the highway, trying not to overthink her being worried. Just a few hours ago, he and Julie had researched vintage engagement rings. He'd found the perfect ring at a nearby auction house. They were having an estate jewelry sale next week, and that ring had Ella's name all over it. They'd make it work. That's what you did when you loved someone, when you chose them every day.

"Okay," he continued. "For the move, it's stressful but it'll be so exciting. And, of course, Eternal Youths can help you with anything you need — boxing things up, driving things to your new apartment. Feeding Pollack. Now tell me more about your mom." He wanted to ask why she hadn't said anything before, why she hadn't told him she'd even gone to visit her mom, but he didn't want her to feel accused and to go on the defensive.

"She... I went to visit her. Okay, yeah, I didn't make a plan but I also haven't seen her in three months and I miss her. I drove to Pinewood and they told me she refused to see me. So... I left. And I haven't heard from her. But I'm worried she won't want to see me before I leave." Ella sounded small. Gideon mulled over what she said while he drove through small side streets, finding the parking lot he was looking for. He parked but left the car on while they finished up their conversation. Unbuckling, he turned to face her.

"Why wouldn't she want to see you?"

"She does this sometimes. I dunno, I think I'm a reminder of reality. But she struggles in reality, so why would she want a reminder?" Ella turned to him, her eyes glassy. "It's just one of those things that hurts, no matter how many times she does it. She's still my mom."

Gideon rested his hand on her knee. He thought of all his conversations with his mom, of all his conversations with Amy. The disappointment he knew he'd brought to his friends and family. He had some understanding of where Margaret was, but it was hard to accept when it hurt the woman he loved.

"I'm really sorry, Ella. There's nothing I can say that will make it better, but I can promise you it will be okay. It will hurt, and it's okay for you to hurt. Just know you don't have to do this alone. I've always been here, and I always will be."

If he could tattoo his promise across every inch of his skin so she could see the truth, he would. But stamping it across his heart was the best he could do.

"Thanks, Gideon. I know you are, I just... I need to be better about being open. Thank you for being patient with me." She held his hand in hers and gave it a squeeze. "Now can we please go eat? I'm starving."

48

Ella held onto Gideon's arm as he led her from the parking lot to a nondescript building off a side street in Poughkeepsie. She did feel better after telling him everything from the past week, but it was weird to know he knew the depth of hurt she was feeling. He was already being softer in the way he touched her, more gentle in the tone of his voice, and she hated it. She didn't want to open up to anyone if it meant they treated her differently. The worst part was Ella was ninety-nine percent sure Gideon had no idea he was doing it.

Gideon held the dark wood door open for her, and she walked into a beautiful marbled lobby. It reminded her of a five-star hotel, warm gold walls and thick red velvet drapes. The desk before her looked like mahogany and sat below an ornate crystal chandelier. The young hostess and the older gentleman beside her looked up, smiling.

"Welcome to Saffron, table for two?" The hostess's dark eyes were rimmed with kohl, her jet black hair in a swinging high ponytail. She was quite possibly the most beautiful woman Ella had ever seen.

"We actually have a reservation, under the name Gideon." His hand snaked around Ella's lower back, pulling her into his side. She relaxed into his support.

"Perfect, come this way." The older gentleman's smile was hidden beneath a thick salt-and-pepper mustache. He led the way down a short hallway behind the desk, pushing open a set of double doors. They entered a hushed room. Dim lighting, tables covered with white linen and crystal glasses. Ella's heels sank into the plush burgundy carpet as they wove between the various patrons on dates, stopping at a small table in the back corner. The man held out Ella's chair before telling them their server would be with them shortly.

Ella surveyed the room. The walls were taupe, the crystal sconces brushing them shades of gold. Curry wafted through the air, the sizzle of one table's dish merging with the soft chatter of its owners. She looked at Gideon. She was excited enough to shove down her feelings from their conversation, to almost forget it had even happened. Besides, he was right. There was nothing she could do but let things happen. It didn't serve any purpose, holding onto feelings or pretending they didn't exist.

She smiled at him. "You have no idea how excited I am. This is so fancy, thank you so much."

"I know how much you love Indian food." He smiled back. "Besides, you've been working hard. You deserve a nice night outside of Sugar Grove."

A small woman appeared out of nowhere, all smiles as she introduced herself. "Hello, my name is Medha and I will be your server this evening. Can I get you anything to drink?"

They placed their order for water before looking at the menu. They picked several dishes to share, telling Medha when she came back with a green glass bottle of water, and went back to talking about the different countries they wanted to visit. Ella couldn't remember the last time they'd talked about nothing in particular, and she realized this was the part of relearning someone that she loved. It'd gotten lost between the conversations of growing, moving, touring, and family.

Medha brought their dishes, the orange chicken

tikka masala radiating the scent of garam masala, the goldenrod aloo gobi steaming. Rice and several plates of naan were placed between them and a third dish, goat-based, arrived shortly after. Ella was salivating, the spices making her stomach grumble.

She *loved* food.

They dished a portion of each entree. The nutty lemon of the coriander in the masala burst on Ella's tongue, the chicken falling apart in her mouth. Gideon had his eyes closed, equally enjoying his food. She watched him dive in, wolfing each bite, and smiled. He made her feel warm, safe. He knew when she needed a night in or a night out. He knew when words weren't enough, and only solace could be found in the placement of his hands or his lips.

Ella watched the man before her, knowing without a doubt they could get through anything. Knowing without a doubt she could spend the rest of her life with him.

49

The drive back to Ella's apartment felt longer than it was. Gideon was full on some of the best Indian food he'd ever had. During dinner, they'd talked about traveling and movies, books and future tattoo ideas. He had his woman, smiling, in the passenger's seat.

The only thing that would make the night better was to get into bed with her.

"Have you heard any more about the festival tour?" Ella's voice broke through his thoughts of kissing her naked body. He readjusted his hardening length while he thought on her question.

"No, we're trying to wrap up the album. We actually ran into a bit of a snag," he said. "With Anthony." She'd been open with him. It was his turn to be open with her.

Ella shifted in her seat to face him. "What do you

mean? Is he okay?" Her voice was laced with concern. Her best friend Julie had had a fling with Anthony last year and, while Gideon was sure Ella wasn't Anthony's biggest fan, he knew her well enough to know she still cared about his well-being.

"He's kind of where I was last year before I got into a program. We had a good talk the other day and he wanted to change, but we were in the studio and he just... stormed out." Gideon glanced at Ella, her mouth hanging open.

"Stormed out?"

Gideon sighed. "I haven't heard from him. Tom called practice for Monday but I also haven't heard anything on his end. Knowing where Anthony is, I'm sure Tom has his hands full."

Silence.

"It is what it is, I'm sure everything's fine." Gideon couldn't tell if he was reassuring her or himself.

Her hand rested on his thigh. "I'm sorry, Gideon. That's tough. If you need anything, please let me know." She gave a little squeeze. "I'm really proud of you and how far you've come."

Gideon covered her hand with his as they drove through the quaint town they called home. Ella's fingers tapped their way up his thigh, brushing his cock. It needed no convincing, standing to attention with the possibility of her wrapping her small hand around him.

"Oh, what is that I felt?" she asked. Out of his periphery, he saw her grin.

Her fingers traced the semi-hard outline, working him until he grew stiff. Her fingers found the button to his pants as he pulled in front of her building. He put the car in park, his mind somewhere else. His pants were undone, her hand on top of his briefs, palming his dick. Ella unbuckled herself and then him, shifting so she was angled toward him.

"How far back does your seat go?" she asked.

Gideon groaned. Her hand never stopped its movement, his cock growing harder with every stroke, needing to fill her. He panted, leaned forward to pull the lever responsible for sliding his seat back. Ella took the opportunity and filled the space between him and the steering wheel, one leg on either side of him, her hand pulling at his tie. Their tongues sparred, claiming the empty spaces. Her dress rode up around her hips. His hands traveled up her thighs and he squeezed, kneading them on his way to the band of her panties.

Except they weren't there.

He pulled away. "You're not wearing underwear."

Ella laughed and kissed her way down his neck, her hand finding his. "No, no I'm not." She moved his hand to her core, placing his fingers at her opening. She was dripping, and he slid two of his fingers into her hot channel. She gasped. Music to his ears. She rode his fingers while his thumb worked her clit, throwing her head back. Gideon's other hand freed her breasts, tweaking each nipple until she cried out. He could feel her muscles clenching around his hand as he brought her closer to the edge.

"I need you inside me." Her words were breathless as she unsheathed his fingers. He fumbled with pulling his dick out, sliding his pants and underwear down around his hips. Ella repositioned above him, her ass bumping the car horn. She folded over him while they laughed together. He held her against him, breathing the sweet earthy smell of her. Gideon kissed her hair, her cheek, reaching for her lips. He wanted every piece of her.

Ella met his lips with hers. Her hand found his cock and placed it at her opening. She slid onto him, moaning against his mouth. Gideon thrust his hips to meet her rocking, the slick movements bringing him closer to falling with her. She leaned her arms against the headrest for balance as they moved faster and faster, her ass bouncing in Gideon's hands while he helped guide her pace. He thrust harder, faster, reaching her inner barrier until she called his name, her muscles milking him until there was nothing left. She fell over him. His arms wrapped around her. Their labored breathing slowed together, the rise and fall of their chests matching.

When she peeled herself off him, he was met with a lazy but satisfied smile. She climbed back into the passenger seat and adjusted her dress. He fixed himself, doing up his pants and straightening his tie.

"Well, that was fun. I haven't had sex in a car since high school." She sighed, staring at him from her seat.

Gideon laughed. "Yeah, me either. What do you say we take it to the bedroom?"

"And the shower?" Her eyes gleamed with the thought.

"We have to get clean somehow." He winked at her, opening the driver's side door. He was going to spend all night taking care of every inch of her body.

He was going to spend the rest of his life taking care of every inch of her heart.

50

The black carpet beneath her feet felt comforting, even if Ella was running it bare from all her pacing. She looked at her phone, the voicemail from her mom staring at her. Asking why she didn't pick up and why she didn't call back.

Gideon had made love to her all night, leaving her that morning with good aches all throughout her body. And her heart. She'd missed her mom's call when she was showering. She'd listened to the message a million times trying to decipher from the tone what mood her mom was in. There wasn't much to go off of, the message just asking Ella to call her back. No apology. No reason why she'd turned Ella away. Pollack lazed on the couch, watching her pace from behind curled paws.

"You're right, Pollack," she said, sighing and

sitting beside him. "I can't put it off forever." She pet his head and he looked up at her, eyes closing. "I just don't know what she's going to say." As soon as the words were out of her mouth, she was hit with the reality that she did know what Margaret would say.

That she'd said the words aloud to Gideon.

But Ella couldn't put it off. She hadn't expected they'd find an office space in the city so quickly, which meant her plans to relocate had been moved up. Which meant she'd have to confront her mom sooner rather than later. She pet Pollack, finding solace in the soft hum of his purring, gathering her wits to make the call. To finally hear the words her mom had always alluded to.

She thought of Gideon's words of comfort and dialed the number for Pinewood. The receptionist answered quickly, her voice sounding distant while she took Ella's name and transferred her to Margaret.

"Hey, honey."

Ella closed her eyes at her voice, choking up from its gentleness. It's mom-ness.

"Hi, mom." She swallowed the lump in her throat and waited for her mom to continue. The silence hung heavy between them. Margaret sighed.

"I'm... sorry. About the other day."

Ella waited, needing more.

"It was a rough one, you know?" Margaret sounded small. "I just... couldn't deal with people."

"Mom..." Ella whispered, clearing her throat to gain clarity. "It's okay to tell me the truth."

It was Margaret's turn to be quiet. Ella didn't know how much time passed before her mom's voice cut through.

"Ella, you know it's not you. It's just hard. Everything makes me want something I can't have. But what comes along with that is the... the disappointment. Namely in myself, but I can't help but think about the disappointment you feel." She sighed. "I think it's better if I remove the disappointment for both of us until I'm in a place to really tackle it. I want this to be the last time I'm here. Truly."

Ella could feel the wet streaks crawling down her cheeks, the need to gasp and sob climbing through her body. She swallowed it down, pushing and pulling the tide within her until she could speak clearly.

"Okay. Just... I'm not disappointed in you, Mom," she said, wiping her eyes. "I just wanted to see you."

Silence.

"I know, honey. And believe me, I want to see you, too. I just need more time."

Ella wrapped her arm around her torso, falling sideways until she was curled on the couch beside her cat.

"Okay," Ella whispered. "Can... Can I see you before I move to the City? I don't know when that'll be exactly, but probably in the next month or two."

Margaret sighed again. "Of course, sweetie. Just call beforehand."

"Will you pick up this time?" Ella couldn't stop the hurt from slipping out. Her mom had a habit of ignoring Ella's calls, and the longer they went without contact, the more likely it was that Margaret would ignore the calls.

"Ella, of course I will." Her mother met ice with ice.

"Promise me."

"Ella, I will."

"Mom, promise me. I need to hear you say it."

Ella waited, curling within herself the longer they went on. Pollack had stopped purring, and the silence, the loss of hope, was an unbearable weight.

"Honey, I promise I will answer your phone call before you leave."

"Okay. Have a good day." She hung up and remained in the stillness. Ella knew her mom thought she was being slick, only promising to answer the phone and not to have a visit. But she was used to these games. She'd have to find a way within herself, again, to surrender and accept that this was her mom. For better or worse.

51

Max and Ryan were pacing around the rehearsal room, nervously glancing at one another.

Anthony still hadn't shown. And neither had Tom.

Gideon chewed his lower lip, leaning against the wall by the window. They hadn't heard anything since Anthony walked out of the recording room last week. And now Anthony and his dad were both absent from band practice.

"K, Tom answered," Lucas said, entering the room from the hallway. They'd all tried calling for the past hour but to no avail. "They're at the Fairfield Memorial Hospital, Ant got into a car accident." Ryan and Max rushed to their coats while Gideon just stared at Lucas, his body going numb, not wanting to think the worst.

"Dude, c'mon. We gotta go." Ryan's voice pulled him out of his stupor, and Gideon looked at his brother. Ryan's face held the same fear Gideon felt, as did Max's and Lucas's. He put on his coat, feeling like he was moving through sludge, and they trudged out into the bracing air to Ryan's van.

The drive was quiet, anxious, the guys keeping to themselves while Ryan navigated their car to the large country hospital. Gideon didn't even realize they'd reached their destination until Max asked if he was coming along, the band already waiting beside the van in the hospital parking lot.

It was a blur getting through reception to the correct lobby, but seeing Tom sitting in the gray chair helped sharpen Gideon's attention. This was real. This was happening.

His uncle looked pale. Worn. The fluorescent lights didn't help, washing out the fake plants and vague artwork to half their normal saturation. The nurses and other patrons were a distant hum outside the circle of Eternal Youths. Or what was left of them, anyway. Tom rose once he saw them and staggered into Gideon's arms. His arms wrapped around Gideon, tightly, and Gideon tried to ignore the warmth spreading across his chest from where Tom was buried. Gideon held on, knowing he had to be the rock Tom had been for him so many times before.

He wasn't sure how long they stood that way, but they separated once Tom's trembling faded. Lucas and Max milled about while Ryan took a seat beside the one Tom had risen from. Tom turned from Gideon, wiping his eyes, and sat back down. Gideon sat beside him, leaning forward to meet Ryan's eyes.

"He's in surgery. He'd... He'd been drinking, and hit a patch of black ice." Tom put his head in his hands, the tears betrayed by the crack in his voice. "He spun in the road and hit a tree head on. They said he was lucky there were no other cars on the road and that they got to him when they did. They said... They said he's lucky to be alive." He broke when he finished, his sobs echoing through the room. Gideon and Ryan rubbed his back, glancing at each other. Max took a seat beside Gideon, and Lucas beside Ryan. Tom stopped his shaking, breathing deeply instead. He looked at each of the guys.

"Thanks for coming guys. They say he'll eventually be okay but... they're not sure about when he'll be able to play." Tom leaned back in his chair, wiping his face. "It'll be another couple of hours until surgery's done. Nothing to do but wait."

Gideon sat beside his uncle, staring into space while the others jumped up to get drinks and snacks for the wait. When they were gone, he turned to Tom, defeat written in his blank stare. Gideon patted his shoulder.

"I saw him about a week ago, and we talked about getting him help. He seemed ready for the change."

Tom sighed. "Yeah, we've talked about it before, too. I really thought..."

He trailed off, but Gideon knew what he was thinking. He'd really thought Anthony would make the change. The rest of the band came back and settled in for the long haul, and they sat in silence while they waited to hear the fate of their brother, and the fate of their band.

52

His text had caught Ella by surprise, and waiting for his response was killing her.

After the conversation with her mom, Ella had managed to pull herself off her couch and move about her life. She'd gotten some work done, spent the night in without drinking or binging Chinese food, and had woken up feeling slightly less depressed. But Gideon's text that afternoon about Anthony being in the hospital stopped her in her tracks. Gideon only said Anthony had been in a car accident and had just gotten out of surgery. She'd texted back asking which hospital but was still waiting.

Patience wasn't her forte.

Ella was trying to keep herself busy with pulling herself together, not knowing what to expect when she got to the hospital. Anthony was her least favorite of Eternal Youths, but she understood his pain and his relationship to Gideon. Which meant she still cared, even if she didn't want to.

By the time she'd finished her hair and minimal makeup, Gideon had responded. Ella threw on the easiest presentable outfit she could find and hopped in her car. She hadn't been to a hospital in years — since a New Year's Eve party when her mom had drank too much — and was trying to reconcile her own personal connection with that of needing to be there for Gideon. The roads were windy, the upcoming winter seen in semi-frozen rivers along the side of the road. Ella managed to only get lost once before getting on the right highway, the county hospital a relatively straight shot from there.

She grabbed the first parking spot she could, squeezing between a large van and a pickup truck. Running to the ER doors, Ella stumbled through the information Gideon had given her to get her visitor's pass, and anxiously stood as the elevator brought her to the right floor. She burst through the doors, seeing the men she'd grown to love sitting in a row. She slowed. Ryan and Lucas were talking in hushed tones while a new guy sat beside Gideon on his phone. Her man was staring off into the distance, his uncle mirroring him. Ella walked toward them, kneeling before Gideon. He looked down at her.

She hadn't seen that look in over a year. Not since the day she'd ended things with him.

"Hey, baby." She spoke gently, her hands going to his knees.

"Hey, darlin'," he whispered. His comforting hands enveloped hers, tears forming in eyes. Gideon stood, pulling her up and into a bear hug. His body swallowed hers. Ella tried to hold him as much as her small body would allow. He was stooped, his arms wrapped around her waist. She didn't know how long they stood that way, but it didn't matter. For him, she'd do anything.

When he finally pulled away, he wiped his hands over his face and sniffled. She didn't know what to say. She rubbed his arm as she passed him, taking a seat beside Tom. She'd had few interactions with his uncle, but he'd always treated her how she expected a father would. Ella leaned her cheek on his shoulder, her hand finding his. Gideon had taken the seat beside her, his hand grabbing hers.

Sometimes people just needed to know they weren't alone.

Gideon had shown her that. He'd taught her that.

And she'd stay by his side — and by the side of the family she'd chosen — while they waited to see where their futures lay.

Thank you for reading the second book in Gideon and Ella's story. Their journey concludes in Finale, book three in the Center Stage series. Find out what happens when things don't go according to plan and their relationship is once again put to the test.

Finale is available wherever books are sold

Did you enjoy this book? Leave a review and let others know!

Find me online:

Facebook
Instagram
Website

Printed in Great Britain
by Amazon